The Phantom of Nantucket

Nancy Drew

DIARIES™

The Phantom of Nantucket

#7

CAROLYN KEENE

Aladdin
NEW YORK LONDON TORONTO SYDNEY NEW DELHI

ALADDIN

An imprint of Simon & Schuster Children's Publishing Division
1230 Avenue of the Americas, New York, NY 10020
This Aladdin paperback edition September 2014
Text copyright © 2014 by Simon & Schuster, Inc.
Cover illustration copyright © 2014 by Erin McGuire
Also available in an Aladdin hardcover edition.
All rights reserved, including the right of reproduction in whole or in part in any form.
ALADDIN is a trademark of Simon & Schuster, Inc., and related logo
is a registered trademark of Simon & Schuster, Inc.
NANCY DREW, NANCY DREW DIARIES, and related logo are
trademarks of Simon & Schuster, Inc.
For information about special discounts for bulk purchases, please contact
Simon & Schuster Special Sales at 1-866-506-1949 or business@simonandschuster.com.
The Simon & Schuster Speakers Bureau can bring authors to your live event.
For more information or to book an event contact the Simon & Schuster Speakers Bureau
at 1-866-248-3049 or visit our website at www.simonspeakers.com.
Cover designed by Karin Paprocki
Interior designed by Mike Rosamilia
The text of this book was set in Adobe Caslon Pro.
Manufactured in the United States of America 0218 OFF
6 8 10 9 7
Library of Congress Control Number 2013954911
ISBN 978-1-4814-0016-9 (hc)
ISBN 978-1-4814-0015-2 (pbk)
ISBN 978-1-4814-0017-6 (eBook)

Contents

Dear Diary,

I CAN'T BELIEVE IT! GEORGE, BESS, AND I are heading to Nantucket, a small island off the coast of Massachusetts. It looks beautiful in the pictures I've seen—very quaint. I can't wait to lie on the beach, eat lobster, and go sailing in the bay.

We're also going to the grand opening of a local museum exhibit arranged by Bess's friend Jenna. Apparently she solved a mystery from the 1800s about why a ship sank right off Nantucket's coast. A girl who solves mysteries . . . I think I'm going to like her!

CHAPTER ONE

~

Ahoy!

"LAND HO!" MY FRIEND GEORGE CALLED, waking me from my nap.

It took me a second to recall where I was, but I grinned as soon as I remembered. I was on a ferryboat headed toward Nantucket Island for a Labor Day weekend of beaches, ice cream, and museums. It had been a busy summer of work and family obligations, and I was looking forward to some time off before the fall.

I sat up straight and looked at where George was pointing. Through the fog, I could just make out the edge of the shoreline and a lighthouse standing tall above the rocks. Painted in bright red-and-white stripes with a glass top that allowed the light to shine through, warning arriving boats of the rocks, it looked exactly how I had hoped it would.

"It's just like a postcard!" I exclaimed.

A voice boomed over the PA system, "We will be docking at the Nantucket Ferry Terminal in approximately twenty minutes. Please take the time now to gather your belongings and clean the area around your seats. Thank you."

I put away the book I had been reading before I drifted off.

"We'd better wake Bess. You know she'll want to put herself together," George said, rolling her eyes.

My best friends Bess Marvin and George Fayne are cousins, but you'd never guess it. They're about as opposite as you can get. Bess isn't a girly-girl, but she likes to wear nice clothes and her hair is always perfectly styled. For this trip, she was wearing seersucker pants, a pink collared shirt, and a yellow V-neck sweater. She fit in seamlessly with the other tourists on the ferry. George, on the other hand, keeps her hair short so she doesn't have to think about it and wears jeans and sneakers every day. I'm more in the middle. I'm not the fashionista that Bess is, but I like to look nice. I guess that's why the three of us are best friends. We all fit together, and we each have our own place.

I shook Bess's shoulder gently, and she woke with a start. "What's happening?" she asked through a yawn.

"We're almost there," I told her.

"Oh, good," Bess said, reaching into her purse and pulling out a hairbrush. "I'm tired of . . . moving."

I knew what she meant. It had been a long trip. We'd left our hometown of River Heights at seven a.m., and now it was almost five p.m. When Bess's mom's oldest friend had invited us all here for the opening of her daughter Jenna's exhibit at the local nautical museum, I hadn't realized just what a journey it would be to get to Nantucket.

"I counted," George said. "We've been on four

different types of transportation today: car to the airport, plane, bus to the dock, and now ferry."

"Maybe Jenna will have bikes we can ride to get that number up to five," I joked.

Bess wrinkled her nose. "I don't think Jenna's the type to ride bikes." She offered George her hairbrush.

"Why not?" George asked, declining the brush. I took it instead.

"She's just someone who really focuses on whatever she has to do. She got straight As in college. Jenna is just an unpaid intern at the museum, but apparently she hasn't been to the beach once all summer. She's spent all her free time in the library! While she was there she made some important discovery, so they gave her a show to curate all by herself. The whole reason her parents can't come to the opening is because they never imagined she would have her own show so soon. They bought tickets to Italy months ago."

We could hear the engines of the ferry slowing. People around us started to get up.

"She sounds intense," I noted.

Bess nodded. "That's a good word for her, but she's also really nice. We're going to have fun this weekend, I promise."

"Ladies and gentlemen, we are docking. We will be disembarking from the starboard side of the ship," boomed a voice from the loudspeaker.

George, Bess, and I exchanged looks. We weren't quite sure which direction starboard was, but everyone around us was headed toward the right side of the ferry, so we followed them. George lagged behind us, lugging her gigantic backpack. She practically staggered as she adjusted to its weight.

"I still don't understand why you felt the need to bring so many electronics with you," Bess commented.

"What else are you supposed to do on vacation?" George asked.

"Oh, I don't know," Bess pondered, "lie on the beach, go for a hike, shop—"

George cut her off right there. "That might be what you do on vacation, but when I'm on vacation,

I play computer games, read on my tablet, see what's happening on the Internet. . . ."

Bess shook her head as she held open the door to the outer deck of the boat. From here we could see people gathering on the dock, waving to the ferry. Walking to the side, Bess peered into the crowd, looking for Jenna.

"There she is!" Bess shouted, waving.

"Which one is she?" I asked.

"Come on, Detective Drew, you can figure it out," Bess joked. My friends like to tease me because in our hometown of River Heights I'm something of an amateur sleuth. A while ago I discovered that I was pretty good at solving mysteries, and now people ask me to help them if they think someone is stealing from their business or cheating in a competition . . . things like that. I scanned the crowd, searching the sea of pastel polo shirts until I saw a serious-looking young woman in a Nantucket Nautical Museum sweatshirt standing with perfect posture, her long brown hair tied back into a tight ponytail.

"I see her!" I exclaimed, pointing.

"You solved the case!" Bess laughed.

"I wish they were all that easy," I joked back, as we walked down the ramp off the boat. I glanced at George. It was unusual for her to be quiet for this long. She was staring down at Jenna, looking slightly nervous. George is always so confident and tough; it hadn't occurred to me that she might be anxious about fitting in with Jenna. Bess and Jenna had known each other their entire lives—their moms had been friends since childhood—but Jenna's family lived several states away from us. Still, Bess's and Jenna's families saw each other every year; they even had a tradition of going skiing together. George and I had heard stories about Jenna for years, but neither of us had ever met her. Originally, Bess's mom had said that my boyfriend, Ned, could come with us to Nantucket, but George had asked me whether it was okay if it was just the three of us. She didn't want to feel like a third wheel with Ned and me and Bess and Jenna. I would have said yes no matter what, but it worked out perfectly, since Ned's family always took their annual camping trip over Labor Day weekend.

"Hello, Bess." Jenna greeted Bess with a stiff hug.

Bess introduced us to Jenna. "This is my cousin George Fayne and our friend Nancy Drew."

Jenna took both of our hands in a firm, business-like shake. "Thank you for coming. It's great to know that the reception won't just be myself and Pete, the museum's director!"

I noticed the baggage cart making its way down the ramp with our luggage. We followed Jenna as she led us to where it would stop.

"I'm sure the reception will be great," I said. "Bess's mom told us you made a really big discovery about a shipwreck?"

Jenna pushed us through the crowd, making sure we would be the first people to get our bags. "It is significant, but you never know how the public will react to something like this, and it's extra important that it go really well. . . ."

Jenna trailed off, and I couldn't help but wonder what she was going to say. That's one problem with being a detective: You can't stand unanswered questions.

"What makes the reception so critical?" I asked.

"Mr. Whitestone, the president of the museum's board of trustees, is coming. If he's impressed by the turnout and the exhibit, Pete says there's a really good chance he'll offer me a permanent position." Despite herself, Jenna broke out into a big smile.

Bess hugged her. "Jenna, that's amazing! This has been your dream job since you were a little girl. Congratulations!"

Jenna put her finger to her lips. "Don't jinx it! It's not a done deal yet. I still need everything to go perfectly tomorrow night."

"Yeah, but it will. I mean, I know you; you've probably checked everything a hundred times already," Bess said.

The baggage carts pulled up and George, Bess, and I retrieved our suitcases. Jenna checked her watch. "The museum is actually just up the street. Do you mind if we stop by before going back to my house? They're hanging a brand-new exhibit banner at five thirty. We could just make it."

"Mind?" Bess said. "We wouldn't miss it!"

We followed Jenna out of the parking lot around the ferry dock, past a row of seafood restaurants, ice-cream parlors, and T-shirt shops. The streets were made of cobblestone and the sidewalks, paved in red brick.

"Is this why people call Nantucket the Little Gray Lady?" I asked Jenna as we passed a row of gray-shingled buildings.

"It's actually because of all the fog, but your reasoning also works," Jenna said with a laugh.

The late-afternoon sun made the whole place aglow with a magical light. With the narrow streets and weathered buildings, there was a real sense that you were walking the same streets that people had walked two hundred years ago.

Bess read my mind. "If it weren't for the cars, I'd almost feel like we'd gone back to the past," she sighed. "It's beautiful."

Jenna nodded. "As a history buff, it's one of the things I love most about this place. It's very dedicated to preserving the past. Take its whaling history. The island was originally settled in 1659 as a whaling colony. Nantucket dominated the trade for almost two hundred years. Given how people feel about whaling now—and the fact that it almost drove whales to extinction—some places might try to hide its association, but Nantucket has a museum with a permanent exhibit on whaling right in the center of town."

"You're definitely going to get that job," George said. "I usually think history is boring. I'm all about the future"—she waved her smartphone in the air—"but you make it seem really cool."

Down the street, a woman who looked to be about Jenna's age walked toward us, pushing a man in a wheelchair. Jenna's face lit up in a big smile, and she waved. The woman stopped, and Jenna introduced us.

"This is Marni, my best friend on Nantucket, and this is her grandfather, Mr. Fraiser," Jenna told us. We all shook hands.

"Mr. Fraiser is my favorite person on the island. Can you guess why?" Jenna asked.

"Because he's the oldest person on the island?" George asked, half under her breath.

"George!" Bess hissed, hitting her.

Jenna laughed. "That's okay. It's true. He's a hundred and four!"

My jaw dropped. I couldn't help it. I'd never met anyone over ninety before.

"Congratulations!" George said.

Mr. Fraiser nodded, but he seemed to be thinking about something else. I couldn't blame him. He was 104. He'd earned the right to think about whatever he wanted.

"Not only that," Jenna continued, "but Marni's family has lived on the island for seven generations."

"Wow," George exclaimed. "You're like island royalty."

"Unfortunately, we don't get crowns," Marni said with a chuckle, "just bragging rights."

Bess checked the time. "Jenna, it's five twenty-seven. We should probably go if we're going to make the banner hanging."

Jenna nodded. "Right."

"We have to head home," Marni said.

A disappointed look flitted across Jenna's face. "You do?" she asked, confused.

"Sorry, Grandpa's pretty tired. The sneak peek at the exhibit earlier wore him out."

Jenna seemed a little upset, but she mustered a smile. "Okay. Well, I hope you liked it. Sorry I had to leave before you finished seeing all of it."

Marni gave a nod. "No problem. Once Grandpa's settled, how about I come join you guys for dinner?"

"Sure," Jenna said. Marni headed off, pushing her grandfather.

"I don't envy her having to push that wheelchair on these cobblestones," I observed. Marni seemed out of breath after only a few steps.

"She's used to it," Jenna said.

We walked quickly, and after two blocks, Jenna stopped us. "Here we are," she said.

We were standing in front of a large brick building. A mural depicting a boat chasing a whale with a harpooner at the ready was on one of the outside walls. It was captioned *Going on the Whale.* Leaning out of a window near the top of the building was a kind-looking middle-aged man hanging a banner.

"Oh good, you're here," the man called down to Jenna. "I was getting worried!"

"You know I wouldn't miss this, Pete!" Jenna yelled back.

Out of the corner of my eye, I saw a guy leaning on the corner of a building, watching Pete hang the banner. The guy kept checking his phone and seemed fidgety.

"Does he look like he's up to something?" I asked Bess, nodding toward the guy.

She laughed. "Nancy, you're on vacation. I order you to relax."

I knew she was right. I was making something into a big deal when nothing had even happened. My brain just wasn't used to not having a case to solve. That man was probably waiting for his date to arrive or something.

Pete looked down at Jenna from the window and gave her a thumbs-up. "Just a few more seconds," he shouted. It took all my willpower not to turn and see how Mr. Fidgety reacted to this news, but I could feel Bess's eyes on me, and I wanted to prove to her that I could be on a real vacation—detective work not included.

"You ready?" Pete shouted at Jenna.

Jenna nodded, turning to Bess. "Can you take a picture on your phone? I know my parents are going to want to see this."

"Of course!" Bess said, getting herself into position.

"On the count of three," Pete yelled down. "One . . . two . . . three."

He unfurled the banner. It dropped down the side of the building, billowing with a satisfying *whoosh*. When it finally fell into place, a gasp went through the crowd that had gathered outside the museum.

The banner advertised MYSTERY OF THE *ELEANORE SHARPE* SOLVED!

But written across it in bright-red letters was the word LIAR!

CHAPTER TWO

~

The Lady Vanishes

"THIS IS OUTRAGEOUS!" PETE BELLOWED as he struggled to rein in the banner.

Whoever painted it had done so recently: The paint hadn't quite dried and was dripping slowly, giving the impression that it had been written in blood. I've seen a lot of disturbing things while solving cases, but even I found the image chilling.

"Who would do something like this?" Jenna asked quietly, her voice catching as she fought back tears.

Immediately, I turned my head toward the suspicious guy I had seen earlier, but he was gone. I thought

I could just make out his back heading down the street, but a thicker crowd was already forming around us. I wasn't going to be able to go after him before he got out of sight.

"Jenna, are you okay?" I heard Bess say urgently next to me.

I turned to see Jenna breathing rapidly and her eyes twitching back and forth as she registered all the people around her snapping photos on their phones. She looked like she was in shock.

The look on her face reminded me of an old friend, Dana from summer camp, who was petrified of heights. One day we went on a hike that required crossing a bridge. When Dana caught sight of the ground and how far away it was, she froze. It had taken us over an hour to get her off the bridge. Later the nurse told us she'd had a panic attack.

Right now Jenna looked exactly like Dana had on that bridge. Her face had lost all its color, and her eyes were glazed with fear, as she inhaled rapidly, as if she couldn't catch her breath.

"Let's get her inside," I urged. Jenna was embarrassed enough already, and I didn't want any more of a scene out here with all these people gathered around. George and I led the way, elbowing through the crowd, clearing a path for Bess to lead Jenna up the museum's steps.

"Jenna," Pete said, opening the door. "It's okay. We'll clean off the sign right away. It will be good as new in no time." He ushered us inside, guiding Jenna into a chair. "Just rest here a moment and catch your breath."

"Kelsey," Pete called to a woman dusting a display of harpoons hanging on the wall. "Can you get Jenna some water, please?"

Kelsey looked from Pete to Jenna for a second, almost like she was deciding whether she was going to protest, but eventually she went with a loud, put-upon sigh. It seemed like a rude response, given how clearly upset Jenna was. Any of us would have been happy to get the water if we knew where it was. Out of habit, I mentally flagged her as a possible suspect before catching myself. This wasn't my case. No one had asked me to look into anything. I was just here as a supportive friend.

Kelsey was taking her time getting the water, but even without it, Jenna looked better already. The color was coming back to her cheeks, and her breathing was slowing down.

I could understand why; the museum felt like a sanctuary. Two of the interior walls were brick, giving the whole place a cozy feeling. The sounds from outside were muffled to a murmur. A scale model of a ship sat in the middle of the room, and a skeleton of a whale hung from the ceiling.

"I knew whales were big," George remarked, a hint of awe in her voice, "but I didn't realize just how big." We don't have a lot of opportunities to see whales (or their skeletons) in River Heights.

I looked up and nodded. From the tip of its beak-like jaw to the end of the tail must have been a good sixty feet—longer than a bus. I felt like an ant in comparison. I couldn't imagine what it would be like to see an actual whale in the ocean.

I glanced at Bess, who was staring at a painting captioned *Nantucket Sleigh Ride*. It showed a whale, harpoon stuck in its back, dragging a ship along as it tried to free itself from the spear. I cringed at the gruesome image. And if I thought it was gruesome, sentimental Bess was probably having a much harder time. Sure enough, I caught her discreetly wiping her eyes.

"Bess," I said, hurrying over. "You know you shouldn't look at things like that."

Bess sniffled. "I know. I didn't realize what it was at first." She followed me away from the painting. "I can't believe anyone ever killed these animals. They're such beautiful beasts."

"Well, if you wanted oil lamps before they invented kerosene, whale oil was the best there was," a voice said from behind us. We turned to see Kelsey standing there, holding Jenna's glass of water.

"It still seems cruel. Whales are extremely intelligent creatures. They didn't deserve to be hunted down," Bess said fiercely.

Kelsey shrugged. "People did what they had to do back then. Who are we to judge them for their choice?"

She crossed over to Jenna, handing her the water without a word. Bess, George, and I exchanged a look. Kelsey didn't seem extraordinarily friendly.

"Feeling better?" I asked Jenna. She nodded. "Do you have any idea who would do something like this?" I prodded, going into detective mode again.

Jenna shook her head. Pete interjected, "It was probably just a prank. The island fills up with kids every summer, they get bored, they see an opportunity to pull off some mischief. . . ." He trailed off.

I nodded.

"'Liar' is kind of a weird thing to write, though," George mused. "What do you think they were saying you were lying about?"

They may tease me, but my friends like a good mystery almost as much as I do.

"I doubt they put much thought into it," Pete said.

Jenna looked up suddenly, turning toward Pete.

"You don't think it had anything to do with that letter we got last week, do you? It said something about us lying, right?"

"What letter?" I asked urgently. If it were just the sign being defaced, I'd agree that it was most likely a prank, but with a letter, it seemed like someone had a vendetta against the museum. That meant there could be future incidents.

"I told you, Jenna," Pete sighed, "we get those letters all the time. At least once a week someone sends us an angry note."

"What do people have to be angry about?" George asked. I was curious about the same thing. It didn't seem like a history museum on a tiny island would be the target of a lot of hate mail.

"Oh, a lot of it is from animal-rights activists who think we glorify whaling," Pete answered. Kelsey, who was hovering nearby, threw a dirty look at Bess. "Sometimes people just had a bad day at the museum and write to us to complain," he continued. "Really, they're not anything to worry about. We've gotten letters like that the entire five years I've worked here, and nothing has ever come of them."

Jenna didn't seem entirely convinced. I wasn't sure I was either.

Pete went on, "Actually, this prank is probably the best thing that could have happened to you and the exhibit."

I could tell that Jenna, who was mid-sip, fought hard not to spit her water out all over Pete. I was surprised too. I couldn't think of any circumstances where being accused of lying would be a good thing.

"How do you figure that?" George asked indignantly.

"Have you ever heard the phrase, 'There's no such thing as bad press'?" Pete asked.

"It's the idea that anything that gets your name out there is good, even if what they say is bad, right?" Jenna asked.

Pete nodded. "Exactly. For us it means that people's curiosity is now piqued. They think there's something scandalous about our exhibit—and everyone loves a good scandal."

I had to admit that there was certain logic to what he was saying. It couldn't be a bad thing to have all those people taking photos on their phones, even if it hadn't seemed like it was good in the moment. They might post the photos on their social media pages, essentially giving the museum and the exhibit free advertising.

"You don't think Mr. Whitestone will be mad?" Jenna asked nervously.

Pete shook his head. "I think he'll be so ecstatic when he sees a packed opening reception that he won't care how we got the people through the doors."

I could see Jenna visibly relax. Pete stood up. "Why don't you show your friends your exhibit? They can give you any last-minute feedback before Mr. Whitestone and the amazing crowds of people you're now going to have see it." He walked into the back room, giving Jenna a reassuring pat on the shoulder as he left.

"See," Kelsey snapped, "even when things go wrong, they still always turn out all right for you, Jenna." She stormed after Pete. Bess stared after her, in disbelief at Kelsey's rudeness.

Jenna gave us an embarrassed smile. "Sorry for all the drama you stepped into. It's usually so quiet here."

"That's okay," I said with a smirk. "We're used to drama following us around."

"I'm going to go wash my face and freshen up," Jenna said, "but then I'll show you the exhibit."

"I'm excited," Bess gushed. "I still remember the exhibits you used to set up with your dolls when you'd make all of us play 'museum' as kids."

Jenna laughed at the memory. "Well, I can promise that this exhibit has cooler artifacts to look at than my beat-up Barbie dolls."

She walked to the bathroom, and immediately George and Bess swarmed around me. "What do you think, Nancy?" George asked. "Is there a mystery here?"

"I'm not sure," I said. "It does seem suspicious that the museum would get a letter and then the sign would get vandalized in the same week, but Pete knows this community better than we do. If he thinks it's just a coincidence . . ." I trailed off.

"I would bet money that Kelsey had something to do with the sign," Bess huffed. "She seems like a thoroughly despicable person."

George and I burst out laughing. Bess always sees the best in people, but if you get on her bad side—usually by treating others badly—watch out!

"I just don't want anything to ruin Jenna's chance at this job," Bess continued, suddenly somber. "This has been her dream for her entire life. She deserves this."

I put my hand on Bess's shoulder. "I promise to keep my eyes peeled for anything suspicious, and if something else happens, we will go into full-on mystery mode, okay?" I asked. Bess nodded in agreement.

Just then Jenna came out of the bathroom looking like the same put-together girl we'd seen on the ferry dock. "You guys ready?" she asked.

"Sure are!" George exclaimed. We followed Jenna as she led us to the back of the museum.

"Do you know anything about the *Eleanore*

Sharpe?" Jenna asked. None of us had ever heard of it. "She was a whaling ship built right here on Nantucket, one of the biggest in the world," Jenna explained. "She brought back more whale oil than any other ship on the island. Her captain was a young, handsome man named Jeffrey Coffin."

"Spooky name," Bess interjected.

Jenna stopped in front of a locked door to a second exhibit space and continued her story. "By the late 1850s, the whaling industry was slowing down. Sperm whales had been overhunted and kerosene had been discovered as a cheaper alternative to whale oil. In 1857 the *Eleanore Sharpe* went out for one final voyage. . . ." She paused dramatically.

We all leaned forward, desperate to hear what happened next. I felt like a little kid huddled around a campfire, listening to a ghost story.

"Whaling trips were long," Jenna continued, "so it was three years before the *Eleanore Sharpe* returned to Nantucket. When the call went out that the ship had been spotted off the coast, everyone in town rushed to greet it. But just fifteen miles from shore, the ship sank as the whole town watched. There were only three survivors, including the captain."

Jenna abruptly stopped.

"So?" George demanded. "What happened? Why'd it sink?"

"That," Jenna said, unlocking the door, "has been a mystery since 1860." She pushed the door open with a dramatic flourish. "Until now."

She turned on the lights, and we stepped inside the room. The walls were covered with paintings of the *Eleanore Sharpe* sinking. Display cases lined the room, housing artifacts that had been retrieved from the wreckage over the years. Worn down by the ocean, they looked otherworldly.

"This is way better than your Barbie dolls," Bess whispered.

"The answer to what happened to the *Eleanore Sharpe* is in this room. See if you can figure it out," Jenna said.

I didn't even get a chance to deduce the answer

before Bess piped up. "Did the captain sink the ship on purpose?" she asked hesitantly, staring at a painting of the captain where he looked downright sinister.

Jenna nodded. "Apparently, he was so distraught about the idea of never going on another whaling trip again, he lost his mind. I'll show you the proof that he sank the ship deliberately," she said. "It's over there."

I looked across to a smaller room that seemed to hold only one display case. Spotlights shone on it from all directions, but I couldn't make out what was inside it.

"Do you know what a figurehead is?" Jenna asked, leading us toward the second room.

"The statue that goes on the front of a boat?" I asked.

"Yep," Jenna answered. She turned around, walking backward like a tour guide. "In some cultures it was believed that a spirit lived inside them, protecting the ship from harm. They're usually just decorative, so it was a real shock that this one turned out to prove that the captain sank the *Eleanore Sharpe* on purpose, thus becoming the key component of our exhibit."

She stopped. "See for yourself." She stepped out of the way so we could take a look, revealing . . . an empty display case!

CHAPTER THREE

~❦~

On the Case!

JENNA TURNED AROUND AND TOOK IN THE empty display case. I glanced at Bess. I was expecting to see her on the edge of tears—she hates seeing people she cares about upset—but instead I saw nothing but steely resolve.

"This is now officially a case," Bess whispered in my ear as Jenna crossed the room to sit on a bench.

"I need to think for a second," Jenna said. She looked completely lost.

I turned to Bess and nodded in agreement. This was a case. The sign and the letter could be coincidences, but a third crime escalated the situation, especially one as serious as this. I was pretty sure that Pete and Mr. Whitestone would feel more comfortable having the police investigate than an amateur sleuth visiting from River Heights, but glances at Bess's and Jenna's faces told me they needed someone to intervene right now.

I walked to the other side of the case and examined the lock. George and Bess followed me. "It's not broken," I whispered.

"Do you think whoever stole the figurehead had keys?" George asked.

I nodded. There couldn't be that many people who had keys to the display case. A wave of butterflies swarmed in my stomach—a feeling that always accompanied a breakthrough in a mystery. We had only one clue so far, but we had already drastically reduced the list of possible suspects.

"Poor Jenna," Bess said, sounding surprisingly disheartened.

"Poor Jenna?" George hissed. "It's great news! Nancy will be able to solve this in no time."

"I haven't been asked to investigate," I reminded George.

Bess still looked uneasy. "This means Jenna probably knows the person who took the figurehead. It was personal. Think about what else they could do!"

I paused for a second. I had been so focused on what it meant for solving the case that I hadn't considered the emotional aspect of what we'd discovered. But Bess was right; it was almost guaranteed that Jenna knew the person who took the figurehead.

"Let's not get ahead of ourselves," I told Bess. "Just because Jenna probably knew the thief doesn't mean that it was a personal attack against her." I had learned over my years of sleuthing that there were millions of reasons why people committed crimes. You never knew the motive until you knew who the culprit was.

"I'd still feel better if we solved this as soon as possible," Bess said.

I took a breath and headed toward the bench where Jenna was sitting, about to ask her who had keys to the display case, when she stood up and announced,

"I need to tell Pete." With that, she set her jaw and marched out of the exhibit room.

My friends and I exchanged a look and trailed after her like ducklings following their mother. Jenna was practically jogging through the museum, past the harpoon displays, the mannequins dressed as traditional whaling captains, and the dioramas of whales in their natural habitat.

"Jeez, she's faster than my mom when there's a sale at the mall," George huffed behind me. I nodded in agreement. Jenna was on a mission, beelining for a door on the opposite side of the building with a big STAFF ONLY sign on it.

She shoved open the door and walked through without missing a step. The door slammed shut in my face. Bess and George almost walked into me, expecting me to follow Jenna, but it seemed like Jenna had forgotten about our existence entirely. I didn't feel comfortable going into a restricted area without an invitation.

We could hear Pete and Jenna talking inside, but

since the door was made of solid oak, I could only hear their voices, not what they were actually saying. Then we heard what was distinctly a sob. It pierced right through the thick door—a heartbreaking noise.

"Oh, forget the sign," Bess said, opening the door and marching in. George and I followed her. I paused for a moment, taking in the room. Clear plastic drawers filled with what I assumed were whale bones lined one wall. The other walls were a jumble of paintings, pieces of carved ivory, and parts of old boats. It reminded me of being in our neighbors Mr. and Mrs. Golon's attic. Mr. Golon was an inventor and Mrs. Golon an artist. They stored all their old inventions and paintings in their attic, which was amazing, but also overwhelming. Jenna was sitting across from Pete, her face in her hands, crying. Pete sat lost in thought, as if trying to figure out the best course of action. A piece of whalebone was on the table in front of him. He had clearly been examining it, as he still wore magnifying goggles that made his eyes look huge.

"Do you want me to call the police?" I asked, pulling out my phone. "I'm sure they'll be able to find the figurehead quickly."

"As soon as we call the police, it will end up in the newspaper as part of the crime blotter," Jenna said between sobs. "Mr. Whitestone will never give the job to someone who lost such an important artifact."

"Sounds like you need a private detective," George piped up.

Jenna nodded, taking her head out of her hands. She looked hopeful at the prospect, but Pete interjected. "It's a good idea, but there aren't any private detectives on Nantucket. It's a sleepy island. There's not much need for someone like that here."

Jenna's hopeful expression fell, but then she noticed the three of us smiling. "Why do you all look so happy?"

"It just so happens that there *is* a private detective on the island," George said, putting her arm around me.

Jenna looked at us, confused. "Nancy?" she asked hesitantly. We nodded.

"Thanks for the offer, girls," Pete said, "but I think we need a professional."

"Well, Nancy just happens to be a professional amateur detective!" George said enthusiastically. Pete didn't look convinced.

Bess noticed too, and explained, "George was making a joke, but seriously, Nancy has solved loads of cases back home. Sometimes the police even ask her to consult."

"Is that true?" Pete asked.

I nodded. "Yes, it's happened a few times," I admitted.

"She's been in the newspaper, and she even won a special commendation from our town," George added.

Jenna looked at Pete hopefully, but he still seemed uncertain.

"She's already had a major breakthrough," Bess chimed in.

I explained my theory that the thief had a key to the display case.

"Based on the evidence so far," Bess said, "it seems like someone is targeting Jenna personally. If that's the situation, having someone closer to her age investigate could be a real asset."

Pete thought about it for a moment. "All right, Nancy," he finally said. "You're on the case."

We made it official by shaking hands.

"I'm going to take a look at the display case myself, see if I notice anything that could be a clue," Pete said.

He walked out, leaving us alone with Jenna. I fished a pad of paper and a pen from my purse. "Can you describe the figurehead for me?"

Jenna thought for a minute before replying. "It's a woman with long hair, about a foot tall and six inches wide."

I nodded, jotting down her description. "Can you write down the names of everyone who has those keys?"

Jenna took the paper and quickly got to work. She seemed to have a glimmer of hope that every-thing would be okay, and I really I hoped I could help.

After a moment Jenna handed back the pad. There

were five names on the list, including herself, Pete, and Kelsey.

"I know who three of these people are, but who are Jack and Megan?" I asked.

"Jack is an outside historical expert the museum hires to help authenticate artifacts, and Megan is one of the restoration artists. They've both gone home for the day, but they'll be here first thing tomorrow morning."

"Can you think of any reason why either of them would want to take the figurehead?"

Jenna shook her head. "They're the most professional people I've ever met. I can't imagine them doing anything like this."

"We couldn't help but notice how rude Kelsey was to you earlier. Could she have done this?"

"Maybe," Jenna paused. "She has been playing pranks on me all summer."

"What kind of pranks?" I asked.

Jenna began rattling off a list of mishaps. "Changing the time of a meeting on my calendar so

I would miss it. Hiding my tools so I couldn't work on an artifact."

"Why doesn't she like you?" George asked.

"Kelsey grew up on the island, living here year-round. I only visit in the summer. There's always a lot of tension between those two groups. People who live here year-round think that summer people are just interlopers and not real islanders," she explained. "Basically, Kelsey thinks I only got this internship and this exhibit because my parents donate to the museum."

"But you've been working for this your whole life," Bess said. "You even won an archaeology scholarship to college. Your parents had nothing to do with your success!"

"I know, but Kelsey was passed over two years in a row for this internship for people less qualified than her, so I understand why she feels the way she does."

"Still, she should judge you as a person and by your individual qualifications," George insisted.

"I'm going to talk to her," I offered. "Even if she

didn't do it, she might have some thoughts about Jack and Megan."

"She's probably in the break room," Jenna said.

After getting directions from Jenna, I headed to the back, thinking about how I would approach Kelsey. Most people think that interrogation is the best way to get information, but I've found that friendliness can be more effective. I thought about what Jenna had said about Kelsey being passed over for people with more connections. I could understand why she would feel angry.

I walked into the break room to see Kelsey frantically digging through her purse, dumping its entire contents on the table.

"Ugh. This day just keeps getting worse and worse!" She sighed exasperatedly.

"What's wrong?" I asked.

"My keys are missing," Kelsey said. "I can't find them anywhere!"

~

CHAPTER FOUR

A Key Discovery

"YOU MEAN ALL YOUR KEYS, INCLUDING THE museum keys, are gone?" I asked. My stomach sank as it dawned on me that my big break in the case might be slipping away.

"Yes," Kelsey answered, still sorting through the contents of her purse. "I keep all my keys on one key chain."

I crossed to the table. "Let me help. Maybe you just need a second pair of eyes to spot them." I sifted through her belongings. I found three lip glosses, two sunglasses, and four half-empty packs of gum, but no keys.

"Are you sure they were in your purse? Maybe

you stuck them in your pocket?" I asked hopefully.

Kelsey rolled her eyes. "These pants don't even have pockets. The keys must have been taken," she said.

"When is the last time you know you had them?" I asked.

"This morning. I also work doing landscaping at the Sailing Club, which is where I was before I came here. This internship is unpaid, and my parents can't afford to cover my expenses." She emphasized the "my," so I knew she was trying to drop a hint that Jenna's parents could. "I'm the first one at the club every morning," Kelsey continued, "so I used the keys to unlock the door, but then I threw them in my bag. I usually don't use them again until I go home at the end of the day."

"And do you keep your bag with you at the Sailing Club, or do you store it in a break room like here?" If Kelsey had the bag with her at the club, then at least I would know the keys were stolen after she left.

"We have lockers. They had to have been stolen on my way here. I walked along Water Street, right after the nine a.m. ferry docked. It was so crowded that I got

jostled all over the place, so I bet I was pickpocketed."
My stomach sank even further. There was almost no
way to narrow down those kinds of suspects. In a span
of five minutes, the case had gone from being virtually
solved to virtually impossible. If I felt disappointed, I
couldn't imagine how crushed Jenna was going to feel
upon hearing the news.

"I gotta go," Kelsey said, gathering everything back
into her purse. "I need to swing by the Sailing Club to
pick up an extra set of keys so I can go to work tomorrow."

She hurried out, and I made my way back through
the museum. I found George and Bess with Jenna and
Pete, going through the *Eleanore Sharpe* exhibit. Bess
and George were checking artifacts off a list as Jenna
and Pete went through every item in the room.

"We're just double-checking that nothing else was
taken," George explained, barely looking up from her list.

"What's wrong?" Bess asked, noticing the disappointed look on my face.

I explained about Kelsey's stolen keys and how it
meant we didn't have any clues. "I'm not giving up,

though!" I said quickly, seeing that Jenna looked absolutely devastated to hear the news.

"What's your next step?" Bess asked.

I pondered for a moment and then turned to Pete. "I think I'd like to see the letters the museum has received. I know you said they're common, but whoever vandalized the sign and took the figurehead clearly wanted attention. I wonder if he or she tried to get it more directly first."

"Sure, if you think it will help," Pete said as he headed toward the door. "Come with me."

Bess and George looked between Jenna and me, not sure what to do. "You two stay here and help Jenna go through the rest of the exhibit," I said. "Knowing if anything else was taken will help us figure out the motive."

I followed Pete into his office, which was crowded with books and papers. In fact, everywhere I looked, there was something shaped like a whale: a pencil cup, a mouse pad, a throw pillow, even a whale-shaped clock on the wall. Pete noticed me observing his collection. "My friends started giving me whale items as a joke when I started this job, but now I collect them in earnest." He paused for a moment. "I just think they're beautiful creatures. Did you know that humpback whales are the only other animals besides humans to use complex grammar in their language?"

"I didn't. That's really impressive." I hesitated for a moment. There was something bothering me. "If you love whales so much, why do you run a museum that shows how we used to hunt them?"

"I think humans have an obligation to face their pasts," Pete explained. "Both the good parts and the bad parts."

That reminded me of something my dad liked to say. "It's like that saying, 'Those who do not learn from history are doomed to repeat it,'" I noted.

"Exactly," he said, lifting a large cardboard file box onto his desk. "But you'll find plenty of people who don't agree with my perspective."

I peered into the box. It was filled to the brim with letters.

"I put all the letters in here," he said. "This represents only the ones we've received over the past six months. Knock yourself out."

Pete headed back out to the exhibit area, and I got to work. I quickly realized that when he said that he put the museum's letters into the box, he meant all of them, not just the threatening ones. I even spotted a water bill in there. I was starting to get the sense that Pete wasn't the most organized person in the world.

The first order of business was to separate the negative letters from the positive ones. I was a little overwhelmed going through this giant box, but Jenna was counting on me. People assume being a detective is exciting and glamorous, but the truth is that sometimes it can be really boring. I pulled out a handful of letters and started reading.

Two hours later I had made my way through the top half of the box. I hadn't found anything that I could positively point to as a clue. Pete was right: The museum did receive a surprising amount of hate mail, but they were all vague. People seemed angry either about the concept of the museum or something very specific that had happened, like their umbrella being stolen or being overcharged at the gift shop. No one said anything about the *Eleanore Sharpe* exhibit or Jenna. Worst of all, the angriest letters were all sent anonymously, so even if I thought a letter had been written by the culprit, I didn't have an easy way of tracking the writer down.

There was a loud knock on the door. "Come in!" I called, grateful for the break. My eyes were swimming.

Marni walked in, a confused expression on her face. "Oh, I thought Jenna was in here. We were supposed to meet for dinner."

I checked my watch. It was half past eight. "Sorry!" I said. "With everything going on, it must have completely slipped our minds. I get like that when I'm on a case. It drives my dad and my boyfriend nuts."

"On a case?" Marni asked.

As I accompanied Marni back to the *Eleanore*

Sharpe exhibit, I brought her up to speed on the missing figurehead.

"I was worried something like this might happen," Marni said.

"Really? Why?" I asked.

"People here—well, the ones who live here full-time—are still really emotional about the *Eleanore Sharpe*."

"But it happened so long ago," I said.

Marni paused, as if trying to figure out the best way to phrase her thought. "It did happen a long time ago, but it's almost like this classic island story, and sometimes people like for a story to remain a story and not be proven wrong."

I thought about what Kelsey had said earlier about the difference between people who lived on the island year-round and people who only came to visit. "Is it worse because Jenna organized the exhibit and she's a summer person?"

Marni nodded. "The captain of that ship is from a family that's important here. It's a big deal to say he deliberately sank the ship. Some people would say it wasn't her place to expose this truth—like it wasn't her story to tell."

I was quiet as we crossed the museum. I wasn't sure how I felt about what Marni was saying. As a detective my job was to uncover the truth about mysteries, which in a way was what Jenna had done. She was like a history detective. Part of me agreed with Jenna that her job was to share her findings. But I also knew that the truth could be messy and hurtful. It could tear people apart. Sometimes people would ask me to solve a crime, but when they found out what really happened, they were more upset and wished they didn't know.

"What about Pete?" I asked. "Is he an islander?"

Marni nodded. "He is. I was a little surprised that he let her go ahead with the exhibit, but Pete loves a good controversy. Anything that brings more people through the door is positive in his eyes."

I thought about how Pete had reacted when the sign had been vandalized and his theory that no publicity was bad publicity.

We found Jenna, Bess, and George checking that all the harpoons were still there. I hadn't realized that going through the exhibits would be such a big job, but looking around the hall again, I was struck by just how jam-packed it was. One artifact could easily be missing and not be noticed unless you were specifically looking for it.

"Oh my gosh!" Jenna exclaimed upon seeing Marni. "I am so sorry. I cannot believe we stood you up for dinner."

"Did someone say dinner!?" George asked excitedly. "I'm starving!"

As if on cue, my stomach growled. "I guess I am too," I confessed, embarrassed.

"I'm so sorry," Jenna repeated. "I am the worst hostess. You come here for a vacation, and I put you to work and forget to feed you."

We all rushed to assure her that we were fine and happy to help.

"It'll probably take me another hour to finish everything here. . . ." Jenna trailed off.

George tried to hide it, but her face fell and my stomach let out another rumble.

"How about I take them to dinner and then back to your place?" Marni suggested. "That way they don't faint from hunger, and you can finish up here."

It took a little bit of convincing, but Jenna ultimately agreed that it was the best plan.

Bess and George returned with me to Pete's office to pack up the letters so I could continue looking at Jenna's house. "Find anything juicy in here?" George asked.

"Not yet," I said. "I'm going to keep searching after dinner."

"We'll help you," George said. Bess nodded in agreement.

I smiled at them. "Thanks," I said, grateful for their support.

We met Marni outside, where a fog had rolled in, making the air damp and chilly. The streetlights cast an eerie glow. I zipped up my jacket. "You can definitely feel that fall is just around the corner," I said with a shiver.

Somewhere in the distance a low moaning echoed.

"What was that?" Bess asked, shuddering. "It sounded like a ghost."

Marni burst out laughing. "It's a foghorn. When it's too foggy for the boats to see the lighthouses, they use horns instead." She looked at her watch. "The last ferry of the evening is going out right now."

"Last ferry of the night?" George yelped. "Does that mean no one can get off the island until the morning?"

Marni nodded.

"What about airplanes?" I asked.

"Nope," Marni said. "They can't fly in this fog."

It was a bit unnerving to think that we were stranded thirty miles out at sea all night. I'd have to tell Ned when we got home. Before we left, he'd laughed that he was off to rough it for the weekend while we were taking a posh vacation. It turned out that in some ways I was more isolated than he was.

"I was thinking we could go to the Harpooners Inn and Restaurant for dinner," Marni said. "It's one of the oldest restaurants on the island."

"Older than your grandfather?"

"At least two hundred years older," she said with a smile.

"I still can't get over it," Bess said. "You said your grandfather is a hundred and four, right? So that means he was born in 1910?"

Marni nodded. "Yep."

"So, he was eight when World War I ended," I realized.

"Yeah," Marni said. "He says he remembers the day they decided to send home the troops, he ran down Main Street waving an American flag."

"That's crazy," George said, impressed.

"He could have even met Civil War vets when he was a kid," Bess mused.

"Or whalers," I added.

"Yes, actually," Marni agreed. "My great-great-grandfather was one of the last of the whaling captains. He raised my grandfather after his parents, my great-grandparents, died."

"I don't think I completely followed all those greats, but it's pretty cool, anyway," George said.

"Thanks," Marni said. "I guess a love of boats runs

in our family. My dad is a ferryboat captain, and I race in the Nantucket Regatta every year."

"What's a regatta?" George asked.

"It's a sailboat race," I explained. "We used to have a mini one at my summer camp, just across the lake and back."

"Yep," Marni said. "I've won the past two years in a row. Right now I'm actually preparing for the fall regatta, which is in a couple of weeks. It's much fiercer competition, so I'm pretty nervous."

"Good luck!" Bess said.

"That sounds more impressive than what we did at camp!" I said.

All of a sudden, out of the fog, a guy emerged, barging right into Bess. "Watch where you're going!" he growled, as he pushed past her, not even bothering to check if she was okay.

"Jerk!" George shouted after him.

"That's the guy I saw acting suspiciously at the sign unveiling," I cried out.

"That's Connor," Marni said with a shrug.

"You know him?" Bess asked Marni.

"Yeah," Marni answered. "He and Jenna dated at the beginning of the summer. They broke up when she said she had to devote all her time to her internship. Connor was really mad about it. He didn't understand why she would care more about the museum than about him."

"Mad enough to try to get revenge on Jenna?" I asked.

Marni thought for a second. "I think so. He's someone who is used to always getting his way, and he gets mad when he doesn't. He came in second at the regatta, and he was so worked up that he knocked over the trophy table, yelling that the whole race had been rigged."

That was enough for me. I turned to follow Connor, but between the crowd and the fog, I couldn't tell where he'd gone. "That guy has a nasty habit of eluding me," I said, scowling.

"Don't worry," Marni reassured me. "He's at the Sailing Club every day, working on his boat."

"Hey," George piped up, "maybe we can check out your winning boat while we're there to talk to Connor."

"I actually don't keep my boat at the Sailing Club,"

Marni said. "Mine's docked in the town marina."

We walked a little farther before stopping in front of a brick building with a wooden sign hanging out front. "We're here," Marni announced, leading us down a small flight of stairs to a cozy, dimly lit restaurant. A fire flickered in a huge fireplace a few feet away. Just like so many places on Nantucket, I immediately felt like I had been transported to a different century. A hostess led us to a wooden booth.

"They say the sign out front is from when this place originally opened," Marni said.

"Is there anything on this island that isn't old?" George grumbled.

"Plenty, actually," Marni said. "If you go farther out of town, there are a lot of new houses and developments. Even some of the houses that look old on the outside have been completely gutted on the inside and redone. There are a lot of fights between developers and preservationists."

"I had no idea that history could be so controversial," I noted. Before Marni could answer, our waitress came and took our order. Bess and I both ordered a cup of clam chowder and a lobster roll, wanting to try the local food. George announced that since lobsters looked like spiders of the ocean, there was no way she was going to eat one. Instead she ended up going with a hamburger.

We ate quickly. I was anxious to get back to the case, and Marni said she needed to make sure her grandfather took all his pills before bed.

Marni dropped us off at Jenna's family's house and gave us a quick tour before heading back to take care of her grandfather. It was a beautiful old house, but we didn't have time to fully explore. Bess, George, and I holed up in Jenna's dad's office and started going through the letters again. At around ten thirty, they announced that they were exhausted and were heading to bed. I only had a few more letters to look over, so I stayed up to finish.

The next thing I knew, someone was shaking me by the shoulder. "Nancy, wake up!" My eyes flew open, and I saw Jenna standing over me.

"Where am I?" I asked, disoriented.

"You fell asleep at my dad's desk," she explained.

I rubbed my eyes, taking a second to get my bearings. I looked at the clock on the wall. It was after midnight. "Are you just getting home now?" I asked.

"I had to go through the whole museum twice after you girls left," Jenna said, sitting down in the armchair in the corner.

"Why?" I asked.

"I discovered that some scrimshaw is missing."

"What's that?" I asked.

"Engraved ivory," Jenna explained. "Whalers used to carve it as a hobby on the boats. There are some really beautiful pieces."

"Do you know when they were taken from the museum?" I asked.

"Based on the dates when the catalog was last updated, it had to be sometime in the past couple of weeks."

At every turn, this case got more and more complicated.

CHAPTER FIVE

The Letter Writer

JENNA AND I WERE BOTH TOO TIRED TO think about what the missing scrimshaw meant for finding the figurehead. We decided to go to bed and regroup in the morning. Tomorrow was going to be a big day no matter what the outcome of my investigation was, and we needed to get some sleep.

I padded upstairs to the room I was sharing with Bess. George liked to stay up till all hours playing on her various gadgets, so we decided she should have her own room. Bess was fast asleep, but she had made up my bed for me. She was always so considerate. I brushed my teeth and collapsed into bed.

The next morning I woke up bright and early, but Bess had gotten up before me. I headed into the kitchen to find her and Jenna sitting at the table, their lips lined with sugar and chocolate.

"Jenna got the most amazing doughnuts," Bess said, licking her lips.

"Help yourself," Jenna said, indicating a brown paper bag on the counter. I reached in and grabbed a chocolate-iced doughnut.

"Ooh, they're still warm," I squealed.

"Yep," Jenna said. "I got to the bakery right as they opened, and these had just come out of the oven. It's something my dad and I used to do. We'd buy doughnuts, then eat them on the docks, looking at all the boats."

"They're really good," I said with my mouth full.

Jenna grinned. "I'm glad you like them. I wanted to show you something good while you were here!" A look of sadness came over her face. I assumed she was thinking about the ruined exhibit. Bess noticed too.

"Jenna was catching me up while you were asleep," Bess said. "She told me about the missing scrimshaw." She turned to look at Jenna to make sure she was getting the word right. Jenna nodded.

I popped the last piece of doughnut in my mouth and sat up straight in my chair, readying myself to get to work.

"Did you work with it at the museum?" I asked.

"No," Jenna said. "I've barely even looked at it. But Kelsey loves it and is quite the expert."

I made a mental note of this. "Is there any specific reason someone would want to steal scrimshaw?" I asked.

"It's pretty valuable and easy to sell," Jenna explained. "It's been illegal to sell new whale ivory since 1973, so the only scrimshaw you can buy or sell has to be vintage. One dealer on the island was actually arrested last summer for selling ivory that was too new. The museum has one of the largest collections of scrimshaw in the world."

I thought for a moment. We'd been assuming all

along that this was about Jenna personally, but maybe the motive was as simple as money. It didn't explain vandalizing the sign, but it was a possibility worth exploring.

"What about the figurehead?" I asked. "Is that worth a lot of money?"

"It's definitely one of the more valuable objects in the museum."

George came in carrying her tablet, and we burst out laughing. Her hair was sticking up in a million directions. She looked like she had a porcupine sitting on top of her head.

"George," Bess admonished, "haven't you ever heard of a comb?"

George halfheartedly ran her hand through her hair, attempting to push it down. "Whatever!" she muttered. "I was too busy reading the paper to comb it. I wanted to see if word of the theft had gotten out, but it hasn't," George assured Jenna, who was looking alarmed at the possibility. "But there is certainly a lot of drama on this island! Check out this letter to the editor." She took a deep breath and started to read out loud: "'Dear Nincompoop Editor: I am writing to respond to yesterday's front-page article about the renovations being done to the 'Sconset Casino. Your reporter says that the project has been held up by unnecessary rules. Those "unnecessary rules" are called due diligence. I suggest you and your idiot reporters look up what that means. . . .'"

George kept reading, but my mind was racing. I quickly got up from the table and rushed out of the kitchen, hustling up the stairs to Jenna's dad's office. I sorted through the letters still spread out on the desk. Finally I found the one I was looking for and ran back to the kitchen.

"Did you find a clue, Nancy?" Bess asked.

I nodded, catching my breath after my sprint through the house. "Listen to this," I said, as I began to read the letter out loud. "'Dear Nincompoop Museum Director: This weekend I had the misfortune of attending the exhibit about whaling ship crews put on by you and your childish staff. Clearly no one could be bothered to do the proper research and due diligence. I suggest your idiot staff look up what that means and stop lying to the public with your poorly researched displays, or you might face some nasty consequences with your next exhibit.'" I stopped reading and looked up at my friends. "This was sent just last week. The *Eleanore Sharpe* exhibit is the next exhibit. Maybe these are the nasty consequences."

"Who wrote that?" Jenna asked excitedly.

"It was sent anonymously," I said, "but it has to be the same person who wrote the letter to the newspaper. There are too many similarities between them. Is that letter signed?" I asked George.

"It was written by someone named Jeremiah Butler," George read off her tablet.

"He's the president of the historical society!" Jenna blurted. "My dad told me he was actually up for Pete's job, but the board thought his exhibit ideas were too dry and boring. Pete's ideas were tourist-friendly and would bring in more visitors. Apparently, Jeremiah didn't take it so well. He even told the board they would regret their decision."

"What if the culprit was targeting Pete, not Jenna?" I asked.

"That could be," Bess said. "Whoever painted the sign and took the figurehead didn't necessarily know that the *Eleanore Sharpe* exhibit was Jenna's project."

"It would be logical to assume that the head of the museum was responsible for it," George added.

"I want to talk to Jeremiah right away," I announced. My friends nodded in agreement. Simultaneously we all pushed back our chairs and headed upstairs to get ready.

"I need a snack first," George said from behind me.

"You ate two doughnuts back at the house!" Bess yelped. George shrugged, but I didn't know why Bess was surprised. We all knew George was a bottomless pit.

We were walking through town on our way to the historical society. Jenna had gone back to the museum to get ready for tonight. There was nothing for her to do except prepare as if everything would go ahead as planned.

It was a beautiful day. The fog had rolled out overnight, and a gentle sea breeze was blowing as gulls circled overhead. All around us everyone seemed to be headed toward the beach or tennis courts.

I spotted a soda fountain across the street. "Do you want to get something there?" I asked George, pointing toward it. She nodded.

Inside, the place was bustling with people both sitting at the counter and placing to-go orders. And like almost everything else on the island, it looked like it belonged in a different century. The front half served food—mostly grilled cheese sandwiches and ice cream, by the look of it. The back was a convenience store, selling everything from beach umbrellas to shampoo.

George read the menu written on a chalkboard behind the counter. "I guess I could get a milkshake," she mused.

"It's nine o'clock in the morning!" Bess barked.

George shrugged. "It has milk in it. That's healthy!"

Bess and I both gave her *Are you serious?* looks.

"Fine," she muttered. "I'll get an egg sandwich." While George got in line, Bess and I hung back, trying to stay out of the way. I was about to suggest to Bess that we wait outside when George gestured urgently for us to join her in line. We fought our way through the crowd over to her.

"Look!" George hissed. "It's Kelsey." I didn't immediately see the significance of running into her. It was such a small island, I'd almost be more surprised if we didn't see her. "I heard the cashier say her card was declined," George added. I looked back at Kelsey. Her face was bright red as she pulled another card from her wallet and handed it over.

"Here, try this one," she said to the cashier, who took it and ran it through the machine. Kelsey nervously tapped her fingers on the counter as she waited to see if it went through. After a moment, the cashier returned with an apologetic look on his face.

"I'm sorry," he said, handing the card back to Kelsey. "This one was also declined." Kelsey blushed an even darker shade of red.

"Sorry," she murmured. "I'm supposed to get paid later today." As she turned to leave, she saw us. Her eyes went wide with fear before she slunk out of the soda fountain without saying a word.

"What payment do you think she's talking about?" I asked my friends.

"You said she works at the Sailing Club, right?" Bess asked. "Maybe it's payday."

"I doubt it," I responded. "It's Saturday. Most jobs don't pay on the weekends." All three of us stood in silence for a moment, trying to puzzle it out. "You know," I said, "Kelsey had access to the scrimshaw all summer, and she would know exactly how much the figurehead is worth."

"And whom to sell it to," George added.

"I'm going to follow her," Bess declared. Before George or I could say anything, Bess had exited the soda fountain and taken off after Kelsey.

"She really has a bee in her bonnet about Kelsey," I observed.

"You know Bess," George said. "She's the sweetest

person you've ever met until you cross someone she cares about."

"That's for sure," I agreed. George was finally at the front of the line. Once she got her food, we continued on our way to the historical society to talk to Jeremiah Butler.

The historical society was housed in a cottage that had been converted into a museum a few blocks off Main Street. Everything about the outside of the house—the condition of the shingles, the paint of the trim, the pruning of the flowers—was impeccable. Whoever took care of the building was a very neat and orderly person.

We walked inside. In contrast to the clutter and excitement of the nautical museum, this place was so clean it almost seemed sterile.

"This is the exhibit?" George whispered to me, pointing to a sign on the wall. It advertised an exhibit on floorboards of houses on the island. The text talked about width and grain and other aspects of the wood, but my eyes glazed over as I tried to read it. If this was

the type of exhibit Jeremiah had pitched to the nautical museum, I could understand why they chose Pete
over him.

"We don't sell T-shirts," a voice growled behind us.
George and I spun around to find an older gentleman,
sporting a long gray beard and a captain's hat, glaring
at us from behind the counter.

"Excuse me?" I asked.

"I figure you girls got lost and thought this was
a place you could shop, but this is not a store and we
don't sell T-shirts." He made a shooing motion with his
hand as if we were annoying gnats. I could feel George
tense up next to me and knew she wanted to tell him
that just because we were girls didn't mean all we did
was shop, but that would get us nowhere. If we wanted
information, we would have to play nice—even if he
wasn't a very pleasant man.

"Are you by any chance Jeremiah Butler?" I asked
as cheerfully as I could muster.

He looked taken aback. "I am. Why?"

"I'm Nancy. I'm a writer with On-the-Go Travel

Guides. This here is George. She's my photographer. We're updating the Nantucket guidebook, and we're going to all the museums on the island."

Jeremiah snorted. "Well, you're standing in the only museum on the island." George and I exchanged confused looks.

"Really? I thought there was a nautical museum." Sometimes pretending to know less than you do is the best way to get someone to talk to you.

Jeremiah snorted again, this time with even more gusto. "That place gives the word 'museum' a bad name. It's a toy store where some of the objects happen not to be for sale."

"This new *Eleanore Sharpe* exhibit seems interesting," I said.

"That's the worst of them! They take a myth, a bedtime story, and shape an entire exhibit around it. What a waste of space! That's not real scholarship. But what can you expect? The director of the museum, Peter Boyd, is a complete nincompoop. And his staff is made up of complete children!"

I was glad Bess wasn't with us. She wouldn't have been able to keep her mouth shut, and our cover would have been blown.

"It's an outrage that the nautical museum won the auction for the figurehead," Jeremiah continued. "It should belong to me. I would have crafted a proper exhibit around it."

I gave George an excited look. Was this a break in the case?

"It must annoy you, then, that the nautical museum is so much more popular," I said, trying to egg him on.

Jeremiah shrugged and for the first time did not look irritated. "The masses always pick the easy option. Genius is often underappreciated."

This man certainly thought highly of himself.

"Anyway," Jeremiah continued, "let me give you the tour, so you can write it up in your guidebook." He pushed back from the desk, and for the first time we saw that he was in a wheelchair, his right leg in a large cast. George and I exchanged a startled glance.

"How long have you been in that?" George squawked.

"About a month. I fell off a ladder while I was repainting the shutters. I was lucky all I broke was my leg." He wheeled ahead and George and I hung back, conferring.

"There's no way he could have stolen the figurehead," George whispered.

"Unless he had someone help him," I offered.

"Pick up the pace, girls!" Jeremiah shouted. "I don't have all day to give you this tour." We reluctantly trailed after him, neither of us looking forward to learning all about floorboards.

Forty-five minutes later we found Bess waiting for us outside. She had followed Kelsey, who had only ended up going back to the museum. Jenna had promised to call us if Kelsey left or anyone suspicious came to visit her at work. We decided to walk along the beach as we figured out which lead to follow next.

"I can't imagine anyone helping Jeremiah," George said. "They'd be bored to death in the process."

"He does seem like a loner," I agreed, "but it's possible that he got someone to help him. I won't take him off the suspect list, but he's definitely not at the top."

A gust of wind came up and swept Bess's hat off her head. She shrieked and all three of us took off after it, but the wind kept it just ahead of us. All of a sudden a hand snatched it out of the sand.

I looked up and saw a strong, good-looking boy holding the hat. "Does this belong to one of you?" he asked.

"That's mine," Bess said, stepping forward. "Thank you for saving it."

"It's never a hassle to help a pretty girl," he said with a smile, holding out his hand. "I'm Mike," he added. Bess took his hand shyly.

"Oh brother," George muttered under her breath. "Another one bites the dust."

Bess didn't mean for this to happen, but boys were just constantly falling head over heels for her. Sure enough, Mike was already making moon-eyes at

Bess. He had reached out to put the hat back on her head when I spotted something: a bright-red paint mark on the side of his shirt.

It was exactly the same shade as the paint used to write "Liar" on the sign!

CHAPTER SIX

❧

Prankster on the Loose

"WHAT HAPPENED TO YOUR SHIRT?" I asked Mike urgently. He twisted around and saw the stain.

"Oh man!" he said, sounding genuinely upset. "This is my favorite shirt!" He stripped it off and ran toward the water. We followed after him.

He waded into the ocean and dunked the shirt in the water, scrubbing at the paint stain. I stood behind him, trying to avoid getting my feet wet. We were on the bay side of the island, so the water was calm, just tiny waves lapping onto the shore. Every once in a while, though, a slightly larger wave would make it farther up on the sand and I'd have to jump back.

"Where do you think it happened?" I shouted over the sound of shrieking children as they played in the ocean.

"Stupid fall regatta," Mike said.

"What does the fall regatta have to do with your shirt?" I asked.

"They're repainting all the mooring stations at the Sailing Club for the fall regatta. I must have bumped into one." He looked down at his shirt. The paint stain didn't look any better. "This is such a bummer. Excuse me, ladies. I have to go find a new shirt."

He walked off, and I turned to Bess and George. "Whoever vandalized the sign probably stole the paint from the Sailing Club."

"Who do we know who has access to the Sailing Club?" George asked.

"Marni said Connor, Jenna's ex-boyfriend, is there every day," I said.

"And Kelsey works there," Bess added.

"To the Sailing Club!" George shouted, throwing her fist in the air. We laughed and trudged across the sand to the parking lot.

"May I see your membership card?"

A middle-aged man with slicked-back hair and a bow tie peered over a counter at George, Bess, and me with a smug grin. He could tell just by looking at us that we didn't have a membership card. I'd known as soon as we'd stepped foot on Sailing Club property that it wasn't going to be as easy to get in as I had thought. The parking lot was filled with fancy cars, and everyone we saw walking in was wearing either tennis whites or fancy clothes. Even Bess was underdressed here—and she looked the nicest of us. George looked down self-consciously. Normally she didn't care about how she looked, but her jeans and dirty sneakers were so out of place, she probably couldn't help but notice.

The man behind the check-in desk was still looking at me expectantly. I had to think fast. "Well, I'm not a member. But," I said quickly, not giving the man the chance to cut us off, "my father is interested in joining. He wants to make sure that I like it before he makes his decision." I added an extra lilt to my voice, trying to come across like a bratty daughter who would throw a fit if I was unhappy with the place. "So," I continued, "can we just take a quick look around?"

"A member needs to sign you in," the man said, completely unimpressed by my story. He turned away from us and went back to his computer. As far as he was concerned, the conversation was over.

George, Bess, and I stepped outside. "Jenna's a member, right?" I asked Bess.

"Yeah," Bess said, "but she seemed really busy. I don't know if she'll be able to step away from the museum."

"I bet if we go around back, there will be a way for us to sneak in," George suggested.

I didn't have a better idea, but it made me nervous.

If we got caught—and I was pretty sure we would—we'd embarrass Jenna and lose valuable time explaining ourselves to security or, worse, the police. I was debating what to do when Marni emerged from a car in the parking lot.

"Hey!" she greeted us cheerfully.

"Are you a member here?" I asked.

"Yep!" She grinned. "Free membership for a year is one of the perks of winning the regatta." She looked at us standing right outside the door, and it must have clicked. "Do you need me to sign you in?"

"Could you please?" I asked.

"Sure. Follow me." She walked inside, with us right behind her. "Hi, Fred!" she acknowledged the man at the desk. "These are my friends. They'll be joining me today."

"I need them to sign here," he grumbled through gritted teeth, roughly shoving the guest log toward us. The three of us signed our names as Fred glowered. George couldn't resist flashing him a self-satisfied smile.

Marni escorted us through the central lounge. White wicker furniture with nautical-themed cushions decorated the area, while small triangular flags hung above. A man in a suit played a piano in the corner. Members walked around us, speaking in soft tones.

"This is the main lounge," Marni said. "The furniture gets put away and it's turned into a ballroom once a month. There's a sit-down restaurant and a snack bar over there. In the back there's Ping-Pong, foosball, and badminton."

"I didn't realize it was so big," I said. "I thought this was just where people kept their boats."

"Yeah," Marni said. "It's a real social hub for summer people. I know a lot of families who are members even though they don't own boats."

"Speaking of boats," Bess said, "I thought you said you kept yours at the marina."

Marni looked uncomfortable. "I do, but Jenna's dad said I could use their boat for the fall regatta. It's a much tougher competition. Their boat is a lot fancier and will really help my odds of winning," she said quickly, almost as if she was defending her decision to use Jenna's family's boat.

"That's great!" Bess exclaimed.

"It's very generous," Marni said. "I haven't decided if I'm going to use it or not."

"Why wouldn't you?" George asked incredulously.

"I just don't know if I feel comfortable," Marni replied. She paused for a second before continuing, "Besides, the GPS is on the fritz. I have to see if I can get that to work before I can make a decision."

"I bet I can fix it!" George offered enthusiastically.

"She's really good with gadgets," I said.

"Don't you need to help Nancy find the figure-head?" Marni asked George.

"Do you mind, Nancy? If you need help, of course I will, but if you two are okay on your own . . ." George gave me a hopeful look. It was a look I couldn't resist, and honestly, Bess and I could handle talking to Connor by ourselves.

"Have fun," I said. George beamed. Marni smiled, still looking a little uneasy.

"Hey, Nancy," Bess said urgently. "There he is!" She nodded toward Connor walking down the hall, holding a Ping-Pong racket. He disappeared through a double door across the room, and we lost sight of him.

"He's probably going to play Ping-Pong," Marni said. "He plays almost every day."

"Bess, how would you like to play a game of Ping-Pong?" I asked.

"I would love to play a game of Ping-Pong," she answered with a smile.

"The rec room is through there and to the right," Marni said, pointing to the double door Connor had gone through.

Bess and I took off after Connor while George headed out with Marni to check out the boat.

The rec room was mostly full of younger kids playing a variety of table games. Others sat in bean-bag chairs, playing video games. We spotted Connor bouncing a Ping-Pong ball on his paddle. Older than anyone else in the room, he looked out of place and lonely.

I nudged Bess forward. "Want to play a game" she asked him with a smile.

Connor's eyes widened. "You want to play with me?" he asked shyly. Bess nodded and crossed to the Ping-Pong table. Connor picked up the other paddle, handed it to Bess, and helped her take off her jacket. Very gentlemanly, I noted. He obviously didn't recognize Bess from their earlier encounter, where he'd bumped into her and spoken to her rudely.

Connor started the rally to determine who would serve first. "Have you ever been to Nantucket before?" he asked.

"Nope, first time," Bess answered.

"How about you?" I interjected.

"Oh, I've been coming here my whole life," he said with a proud smile.

"So you must know our friend Jenna. She's been coming here her whole life too," I offered, as if I didn't know anything about his and Jenna's history.

Connor's face hardened. He glared at me icily and then looked suspiciously at Bess. "What is this?"

I shrugged. Connor stared at me. He could tell that I knew more than I was saying.

"If you were really friends with Jenna," he continued, "you would know that she and I are not on the best of terms right now."

It was time to drop my act.

"Someone's going after Jenna," I said. "And as far as I can tell, you're the only person who has a problem with her."

To my surprise, Connor started laughing. "What a baby! She freaks out and sics her friends on me because of one tiny prank?"

"It was a pretty big 'prank,'" Bess stated.

"I'm glad you two were impressed, but it really wasn't that big of a deal. I just took some paint and wrote 'Liar' on her precious sign. She is a liar. She said she cared about me," Connor snarled.

"And then when everyone was distracted by the sign, you took the figurehead?" I asked.

"Someone took her figurehead?" he asked. "She must be flipping out!"

Bess scowled. "I thought you cared about Jenna!"

"If she doesn't care about me, I don't care about her," he replied.

I still had more questions for Connor. I wasn't sure I believed that he had nothing to do with the figurehead. So far he had the strongest motive, and he clearly had a temper. Before I could ask anything else, Marni came running into the rec room, a frantic look in her eyes.

"Nancy! Bess! You need to come right now!"

"What happened?" I asked.

"There's been an accident," Marni said, her lips quivering as she fought back tears.

Bess and I turned and looked at each other, our eyes wide with fear.

"George!" we yelled.

CHAPTER SEVEN

Overboard

"THE NURSE THINKS SHE MIGHT HAVE A concussion," Marni said in a shaky voice as she led us through the club to the nurse's office.

"A concussion?" Bess asked. I could hear how scared she was. "That's a brain injury, right?"

Marni nodded. "The nurse is running some tests here, but George might have to go the hospital for more."

I gulped, working hard to fight back tears. George was always so tough and unafraid that it was hard to imagine her seriously hurt. I tried to prepare myself for the worst before we saw her.

"How did this happen?" I asked.

"The boom slipped and it hit George on the back of the head, knocking her overboard. I jumped in and got her out," Marni explained.

Bess stopped and wrapped Marni in a giant hug. "You saved her life!" Bess burst out.

Marni looked embarrassed. "It was no big deal. I used to work as a lifeguard." She tried to extract herself from Bess's grasp, but Bess wouldn't let go.

"No, it is a big deal. You're a hero," Bess said emphatically. Marni blushed and looked uncomfortable at the attention. I interjected with some questions to help change the topic.

"If I remember my sailing lessons from summer camp, the boom is the horizontal pole that holds the sail, right?" I asked.

Marni nodded.

"But how did it get loose?" I wondered out loud.

"The knot slipped. I don't know how," Marni said as we reached the door to the nurse's office. We barged in to find George sitting on the exam table with a towel draped around her. Her clothes were sopping wet. The nurse stood in front of her, holding up two fingers.

"How many fingers do you see?" the nurse asked. George stared at the fingers, squinting her eyes as if she was trying to focus. Bess squeezed my hand. I squeezed back and held my breath as I waited for her to answer. What was taking her so long? Could she really not see how many fingers the nurse was showing her?

"Four?" George finally answered hesitantly. I gulped loudly. Bess's breath caught in her throat. The nurse turned to us with a concerned expression on her face.

"Just kidding!" George shouted, laughing. "Two! It'll take a lot harder hit than that to injure this brain."

"If I weren't so happy you were okay, I'd shake you for scaring us like that. It wasn't funny!" Bess scolded her.

The nurse handed George an ice pack. "Keep that on there for at least twenty minutes." She turned to Bess and me. "If she starts feeling dizzy or like she's going to throw up, you need to take her to the hospital right away."

We nodded. I knew Bess would watch George like a hawk and take her to the emergency room if she so much as put her hand on her stomach.

"All in all," the nurse continued to George, "you are a very lucky young lady. This could have easily been much, much worse."

"Don't I know it?" George smiled. "Usually I keep my phone in my pocket, but I took it out to take a selfie of myself behind the captain's wheel, and I left it on the console. She paused for a moment, shaking her head. "If my phone had gone overboard with me, that would have been a real disaster!"

"She's fine!" I said with a laugh. Even the nurse smiled.

"Is your phone still on the boat?" Marni asked. She was still standing at the back of the office. I'd been so focused on George and making sure she was okay that I'd completely forgotten Marni was in the room.

"It had better be!" George said.

"I'll get it for you," Marni offered.

"And I'll find you some dry clothes," Bess suggested.

They both left the room. I had some questions for Marni about exactly what had happened on the boat. "George, will you be okay if I leave you alone for a few minutes?"

"Sure. I'll be fine," George answered.

I exited the nurse's office and saw Marni at the end of the hallway. "Marni," I called out. "Wait up!" She slowed down and I caught up to her.

"I just wanted to go over what happened one more time."

Marni looked around nervously. "I don't know. All of a sudden the knot just slipped and the boom went swinging and hit George. It happened so fast, I couldn't do anything to stop it."

"It's not your fault," I tried to assure her. "Accidents happen."

Marni bit her lip. "I'm not so sure about that."

I stepped in to stand closer to her and lowered my voice. "What do you mean?"

"I don't have any proof or anything, you know, but . . ." She trailed off.

"You have a hunch?" I asked.

Marni nodded. "The thing is, the knot that was used to tie the boom is really reliable. It almost never slips. There's a reason sailors use it."

"What are you saying?" I asked.

Marni took a deep breath. "I think someone tampered with the knot."

My mind raced through all the implications of this information. The biggest question, of course, was, who was the target of the sabotage? Maybe the thief knew George was helping me with the case? George had gone onboard so spontaneously, I couldn't see how the culprit would have had enough time to mess with the knot without Marni and George seeing them. Maybe this was entirely unrelated to the theft of the figurehead.

"Do you think someone was trying to hurt you so you couldn't compete in the fall regatta?" I asked Marni.

"That's the thing," Marni said. "No one knew about Jenna's family lending me their boat."

It took me a moment, but suddenly I understood what she was implying. "You think someone was trying to hurt Jenna?" I asked.

Marni nodded glumly. "I don't mean to be a bad friend, but I'm starting to think Jenna should cancel her exhibit. It's not worth getting hurt."

I understood why Marni would say that, but I didn't want to give up yet. "I'm going to come with you to the boat," I said.

"Are you sure?" Marni asked. "It might not be safe. Whoever messed with the knot might have sabotaged something else."

"That's what I'm counting on," I said. Marni looked confused. "The more things a culprit touches, the more chances they left behind a clue," I explained. Marni still looked nervous, but she agreed and we headed to the boat.

We cut across the well-groomed lawn to the docks and made our way down to the last slip. Even with my limited knowledge of boats, I could tell this was an impressive one. It looked sleek and powerful, like it could cut through water at a quick pace.

"This is it," Marni said. "The *Mayflower*."

"Like the boat the Pilgrims came to America on?" I asked. Marni nodded.

"Did Jenna name it?" I asked with a grin.

Marni laughed. "She does have a bit of a one-track mind: history, history, history. Sometimes it can be difficult to get her to focus on the present."

She walked to a large box at the end of the dock and pulled out a bright-orange life jacket. "Put this on," she said. "Even though we're not leaving the dock, I'm not taking any chances."

I took the life vest and clipped it on. I felt silly, but I knew Marni was right. If someone was booby-trapping the boat to cause Jenna bodily harm, then we couldn't be too careful. Once my life jacket was secure, we climbed onboard the *Mayflower*. Even docked, there was a gentle sway to the boat that took some getting used to. Marni led me to where the boom was tied up.

"Okay," she said. "I just tied this knot after the old one slipped. This is what it's supposed to look like." I studied the knot, the way the rope twisted and turned on itself. "You should be able to tug on it like this," she demonstrated, "and it shouldn't budge." I tried it. She was right. The knot didn't move.

"That's incredible," I said.

"It is pretty amazing what you can do with the right knot," Marni agreed. She walked over to a pile of extra canvas for the sail that was sitting near the back of the boat. "You want to check the other knots and look for clues? I'm going to move this to the hull. If someone is messing with the boat, I want as much locked belowdecks as possible." She struggled to pick up the pile of canvas.

"Here, I can help you," I said, rushing over to her.

"I've got it," Marni grunted. She maneuvered past me. I could hear that her breathing was strained as she made her way down the stairs.

I shook my head. These islanders really were tough. I guess living thirty miles away from the rest of civilization made you self-reliant.

I checked all the knots, but they were all tied correctly. Then I scoured the deck for clues. Nothing appeared out of place. I sighed. I had really hoped to find a lead on the boat.

Marni said all the instruments checked out. We grabbed George's phone and headed back to the nurse's station. We walked back in silence, both lost in our own worlds.

When we arrived, we found Bess sitting in a chair, her arms crossed in annoyance. George was nowhere in sight.

"Where's George?" I asked.

Bess indicated the closed bathroom door. "She refuses to come out."

"No one can see me like this," George yelled through the door.

"I told you," Bess answered. "That's all they had."

"Then just give me back my wet clothes!" George yelled.

"You're not getting sick on top of a head injury," Bess hollered back.

I've known George and Bess long enough to know they were in a standoff and neither was going to budge unless someone intervened.

"Hey, George," I called out. "I have your phone." Almost immediately, the bathroom door creaked open and George padded out. If not for the furious glare she was shooting me, I would have burst out laughing. Apparently the only clothing Bess could find for George was the Sailing Club's waitress uniform. George was decked out in a khaki pleated skirt and pink collared shirt that bore the Sailing Club insignia. I could not imagine a more un-George-like outfit.

"May I have my phone, please?" George said, still sulking.

I handed the phone over. "Okay, so the outfit isn't exactly you, but you don't look bad," I said gently, trying to make her feel better.

"Thanks," George muttered, quickly immersing herself in her phone and everything she had missed in the thirty minutes she had been separated from the Internet.

I sat next to Bess and Marni and recounted our theory that the boat accident had been intended for Jenna.

"Nancy," Bess said seriously, "I know this would be bad for Jenna's career, but I think it might be time to go to the police. If she's physically in danger . . ." She left the rest unspoken, but I knew what she was getting at. And she was right. Jenna's job being at stake was one thing, but her safety was another. It was probably time to bring in the professionals. It was frustrating because I knew I was close, but maybe not close enough. I had lots of leads, but no solid evidence indicating the culprit. Who knew what could happen to Jenna while I was struggling to make sense of all the pieces?

"Guys!" George said abruptly. "We need to go back to the museum right now."

"Why? What's going on?" Bess and I asked.

"The newspaper just posted that an anonymous source told them there was a theft at the museum affecting the *Eleanore Sharpe* exhibit. It's not a secret anymore!" George said.

CHAPTER EIGHT

⁓

A Man with a Past

BESS, GEORGE, MARNI, AND I WALKED BACK to the museum as fast as we could. "Poor Jenna," Bess moaned.

I wondered if Connor had leaked the information to the press after I'd let it slip to him that the figurehead was missing. I was really botching this case! I was going to have to apologize profusely to Jenna.

We turned the corner onto Broad Street from Beach Street. Half a block ahead a large crowd had gathered on the sidewalk in front of the museum.

"What do you think is going on?" Bess asked.

None of us had an answer. Without saying a word, the four of us picked up our pace.

Even closer to the action, it was still hard to figure out exactly what was happening, but people were in line, pushing and shoving to get to the front. Amid all the yelling, I could make out people shouting about tickets.

I tapped the shoulder of the man directly in front of me. "What's going on?" I shouted over the noise.

"Apparently, there's been a robbery at the museum! We're all buying tickets to the opening reception tonight."

I still didn't follow. "Why would you want tickets if there's been a theft?"

The man looked at me like I was dumb. A woman behind me leaned over my shoulder. "First the sign, now the theft," she said. "Something big is going to happen at this reception, and I am going to be here to see what it is!"

The man in front of me nodded in agreement. "This is going to be the biggest story on the island tomorrow morning. Everybody who's anybody will be there."

"So you're trying to get tickets to see something bad happen at the museum so you can gossip about it?" I asked, making sure I understood what they were saying. Both the man and the woman nodded. I stormed back to my friends, furious. Jenna had worked so hard on this exhibit, and now all these people just wanted to see her fail. "Let's find Jenna," I said.

Marni checked the time. "I gotta go," she said. "My grandfather and I play chess every Saturday afternoon."

"Okay," I said. "We'll see you at the reception." Marni nodded before heading off.

"I think it's great how close she is with her grandfather," Bess observed. I agreed. It was nice to see.

"Ugh, this thing is leaking," George muttered, holding out the ice pack with water running down her arm.

Bess glared at her. "Don't you dare take that off your head," she said sternly.

"It's been twenty minutes!" George protested as she found a trash can and threw it away.

We pushed our way through the crowd and up the stairs to the entrance. We did a quick search of the museum but didn't spot Jenna.

"I'll text her," Bess offered.

"I'm going to the bathroom while we wait," George announced.

After a moment, Jenna responded that they were in the staff room, and George emerged from the bathroom in her normal clothes.

"George!" Bess said.

"They're barely damp," George countered. Bess tugged at George's clothes and grudgingly agreed.

"Are we all set?" I asked. The girls nodded and we made our way to the staff room. Both Pete and Jenna were there. Jenna looked completely spent. She was slumped in a chair, her face pale and gaunt. I couldn't blame her. Her worst fears were coming true. Pete, on the other hand, was pacing, full of energy, like a kid after eating an entire bag of Halloween candy.

"Nancy Drew, the girl detective!" he greeted me with a big smile on his face.

"You seem happier than I expected," I said.

"Have you seen the crowds outside?" he asked, beaming. "We haven't had this much attention about any of our exhibits in years." He turned to Jenna. "Was I right about the power of negative publicity or what?"

Jenna gave him a wan smile. "But now there's no hiding it from Mr. Whitestone. He'll know we lost the figurehead."

"That's not true," Pete said. "Right now all the newspaper has is a rumor. They have no proof that anything is missing. As long as the figurehead is back by the time he arrives, Mr. Whitestone will just commend us for turning out such a big crowd. He won't care how we did it." I knew then that Pete wasn't going to call the police, and he definitely wasn't going to close the exhibit. He loved the excitement and the attention this was bringing. So far this was all good news for the museum.

His phone rang, and he stepped away to answer it. "I'll be right there," he said, turning back to us. "They need my help selling tickets up front," he told us, beaming. He looked directly at me as he left the room. "Nancy, my dear. I am counting on you. Find that figurehead!"

"He's very optimistic about how all this will work out." I said, not understanding why Pete wasn't more concerned.

"That's just Pete," Jenna said with a sigh. "He always believes in people. It's why he gave me this chance in the first place. Most museum directors would never have given me this opportunity. Maybe they'd be right."

"No," Bess said firmly. "You did a terrific job. We're going to figure this out. Nancy has a lot of leads. We just need to finish tracking them all down." My stomach sank. I had a lot of leads, but no sense of where they went. I hoped Bess wasn't giving Jenna false hope.

"Who are your top suspects?" Jenna asked.

"All right," I said. George whipped out her laptop and started to take notes. "Kelsey is still a suspect," I said. "You two have a history. She would directly benefit from you not getting the job. If her keys really were stolen, though, she didn't have a way of accessing the display case."

"Who else could it be?" Jenna asked.

"There's Jeremiah Butler. He would love to see Pete and the museum embarrassed, plus he admitted that he wanted the figurehead for his own museum."

"But he's in a wheelchair," George noted.

"Right," I said, "so if it is him, he's not working alone."

"Anyone else?" Jenna asked.

"There's also Connor," I said.

"Connor?" Jenna said, surprised. "I knew he was mad at me, but I didn't think he would do something like this."

"Well, he confessed to vandalizing the sign. He denied knowing anything about the figurehead, but sometimes a suspect confesses to a smaller crime to throw suspicion off themselves for the bigger one."

Jenna shook her head. "I can't believe I ever liked him."

"Do you think he would be capable of taking the

figurehead as well as vandalizing the sign?" I asked.

Jenna thought hard. "I wish I could say no, but he has a vindictive side."

"Marni told us that at the regatta this summer he knocked over the trophy table when he came in second," Bess mentioned.

"It was worse than that," Jenna muttered. "After he knocked over the table, he picked up the first-place trophy and stomped on it right in front of Marni. He told her it was worthless and she didn't deserve it because she cheated. But Marni didn't cheat; she was just better than he was."

"Did he know how important the figurehead was to the exhibit and to you?" I asked.

"Definitely," Jenna replied. "I had just discovered it when I called it off with him to spend more time restoring it. I think he blames the figurehead for our breakup."

"All of these seem like strong suspects," George agreed. "But how do we figure out which one actually stole it?"

I was quiet for a moment, considering my answer.

The truth was I wasn't sure. Something felt off. Usually when I'm working on a case, the solution suddenly snaps into focus, but this one still seemed blurry. Even though Kelsey and Connor were strong suspects, I didn't think either of them had stolen the figurehead. All of Connor's other actions had been spontaneous, motivated by a clear moment of anger. To steal the figurehead would have taken consideration and planning. That didn't seem like Connor. My interactions with Kelsey made me think that she wanted to make it on her own, not take someone else down to get ahead. She might be bitter and jealous, but I didn't think she would feel satisfied if Jenna failed because of sabotage. Jeremiah seemed like such a loner, it was hard to imagine him working with a partner.

Before I could explain any of this to my friends, Kelsey walked in. She sat down, ignoring Bess, George, and me, and turned to Jenna. "Break's over. It's your turn to usher."

We followed Jenna out of the staff room and into

the main museum area. She picked up a stack of maps and stood near the entrance. All of a sudden, I felt my phone buzz in my purse. I checked the caller ID. It was Ned!

"Hello?" I answered, stepping outside so I wouldn't bother the museum patrons. "I thought you didn't have cell service in the woods," I said, confused. "Is everything okay?"

"Yeah, everything's fine. It was raining cats and dogs the whole time, so we decided to pack it in. How about you? I thought you'd be swimming in the ocean right about now. I was just going to leave you a message to let you know I was home."

"I haven't really had a chance to go swimming yet," I said.

My boyfriend seemed to immediately know why. "Nancy, did you find yourself a case?"

I filled him on what was going on and ran down the list of suspects.

"This might sound weird, but do you think Jenna could have taken the figurehead herself?" he asked.

"Why would she do that?" I replied.

"Having your own exhibit is a lot of pressure, especially with a job riding on it," Ned pointed out. "Maybe she couldn't take it and couldn't think of any other way to cancel the exhibit. We've seen it before."

That was true. I had solved cases where the culprit turned out to be the same person who'd hired me. "I'll look into it," I said. "Thanks for listening to me."

"Anytime."

We said our good-byes, and I headed back inside the museum. I was still lost in thought when two middle-aged women walked by me. They wore matching skirt suits—one in red, the other in yellow—and they both clasped purses that were actually baskets made out of woven wood with ivory on top. One look at their faces told me they had to be sisters.

"This is so like Pete," one said to the other.

"Tell me about it. Only he would fake a theft to sell tickets to his opening-night reception."

I quickly caught up to the sisters. "Excuse me," I said. "I couldn't help but overhear what you said.

What do you mean Pete would fake a theft?"

The women exchanged a look and then leaned in close. "You've heard these rumors about the theft, I assume?" the one in red murmured.

I nodded.

"Well, that's all it is, dear, a rumor. A new, ingenious way for Pete to sell more tickets!"

"He's done this before?" I asked.

"Well, not this exact ruse, but similar schemes," said the one in yellow.

"Like what?" I asked.

The ladies led me over to a bench. I knew this was going to be a long story, but I was all ears. "Pete's father started the Nantucket Ghost Tour," the one in red said.

"You've probably seen it around," the other chimed in. "They take you on a walk around town to a bunch of different houses and hotels and tell you how they're haunted—all a bunch of hooey. Until he left for college, Pete's job every summer was to sell tickets."

"He'd sit at one end of Main Street in a top hat," the red sister interjected, "wearing a sign over him. He had to fill the tours. His family depended on him to sell out the tours in order to have enough food on the table. That boy learned how to say and do anything to sell a ticket."

"He'd spin these yarns about how his mother had passed away when he was born and that's when he began to see ghosts," the sister in yellow said, pausing for dramatic effect. "Pete's mother is alive and healthy as a horse today!"

My jaw dropped. If Pete was capable of that, what else might he be capable of? Hiding the figurehead and telling the press it was stolen to create more buzz around the exhibit didn't seem too far-fetched. If that was his plan, it had certainly worked! It would also explain why he was so confident that the figurehead would return in time.

I felt excited to have a new lead to pursue after going in circles for so long. I just needed to prove for sure that he had taken it so I could tell Jenna not to worry.

Just then I saw Jenna walk by with a concerned

expression on her face, gesturing for me to come over. "Nancy," she whispered urgently in my ear. "Look at her brooch!"

The sister in red had an ivory brooch pinned to her suit jacket; the brooch had been carved to depict a whale breaching, with a whaling ship in the background.

"What about it?" I asked Jenna.

"That's one of the pieces of scrimshaw that was stolen from the museum!" she hissed.

~

CHAPTER NINE

Brooching the Subject

"IF WE CAN FIND OUT WHERE SHE GOT THE brooch, we might be able to track down who stole it in the first place," I whispered excitedly to Jenna.

"If they stole the scrimshaw, they probably stole the figurehead, too!" Jenna said.

She and I walked back over to the sisters, who were chatting quietly. "Excuse me, ma'am," I said to the one in red. She looked over, mildly annoyed to be interrupted.

"Yes, dear?" she asked.

"That is a beautiful brooch. I've been thinking

about what kind of souvenir I'd like to buy to remind me of my trip, and I think I'd like a brooch like yours. Could you tell me where you got it?"

"Let's see, which one am I wearing today?" the woman murmured to herself, looking down at her lapel. "Oh, this one. Sorry, girls. I've had this for years. It's an old family heirloom that was passed down from my mother." I looked at Jenna, confused.

"I know that's the one that was stolen," Jenna whispered to me. "I stared at its photo in our catalog for hours last night. See the chip missing on the top left sail? That's our scrimshaw."

I looked over. She was right; there was a chip in the sail. I doubted that could be a coincidence, though I also didn't think this old woman had stolen the scrimshaw. She was probably confused, but I wasn't sure how to tell her this was not her beloved family heirloom.

Thankfully, the sister in yellow interjected. "That's not the brooch you got from Mother!" she said sharply.

"Yes, it is!" her sister answered defensively.

"No," the other insisted. "The one you got from

Mom has a humpback whale. That brooch has a sperm whale."

"Let me see." The sister in red pulled out a pair of glasses and put them on, studying the brooch.

Beside me, Jenna tapped her foot impatiently. I shared her agitation, but I knew that rushing this woman would just fluster her and make her take longer. As much as we wished we could hurry her along, we had to let her go at her own pace.

"Oh, you're right," the sister said. "This isn't the one from Mother."

"She should have given the brooch to me," the one in yellow muttered under her breath. "You never did appreciate her gifts."

The sister in red lifted her head sharply. Her eyes narrowed as she prepared to answer back. I don't have any siblings, but I knew this was the kind of argument that could get out of control very quickly.

"Can you remember where you got it?" I interrupted, trying to keep us on track.

"Let me think for a second," the woman said,

distracted from her sister for the moment. She scrunched her eyes, trying to remember. I crossed my fingers behind my back, hoping that it would come back to her. This was our first solid lead, and I needed it to come through. Otherwise I was running out of ideas for how to find the figurehead. I had no proof with which to confront Kelsey, Connor, Jeremiah, or now possibly Pete.

"You probably got it at that little antique shop on India Street you like so much," the sister in yellow said impatiently.

"Yes, you're right!" the other exclaimed. "I did buy it there. I remember now. It's a lovely place. They have the best scrimshaw collection on the island."

"It really is beautiful," I said, standing up now that I had the information I needed. I looked at Jenna. "Do you know the antique store she means?"

Jenna nodded. "Yes, it's called Captain Jim's Treasure Chest."

"Let's go," I told her. I turned back to the ladies. "Thank you for your time." I always try to be polite when on a case—and in everyday life, too, but especially during a case. You never know when you might need to ask someone for more information later. If you're rude or take them for granted, they might not want to help you again.

Jenna and I went to grab her purse from the staff room and found Bess and George sitting in the corner.

"Do you feel dizzy?" Bess asked.

"No," George said.

"Are you sure? Not even a little bit light-headed?" Bess pushed.

"The only thing I feel is annoyed that you won't stop pestering me," George insisted. This case was getting to all of us. We were cranky and frustrated.

As soon as I filled them in about the stolen scrimshaw and the old woman telling us where she'd bought it, Bess and George perked up.

"What are we waiting for?" George said, jumping up from her seat. Bess rolled her eyes, but she knew that getting her cousin to slow down was a next-to-impossible task. Jenna got her purse and we headed out of the museum and down Bond Street.

"What time is it?" Jenna asked.

"Four fifty-two," George said.

"I'm pretty sure they close at five," Jenna said.

"Run!" I said. Jenna took off, leading the way. It was only six blocks away, but by the time we arrived, we were all panting and out of breath. We stood for a second, trying to regain our composure. Just as we were about to go in, a woman came to the door and flipped the sign to CLOSED.

We all looked at each other. Then I sprang into action, running to the door and knocking loudly. The lady returned with an irritated look on her face. She opened the door a crack, just enough to be able to talk to me. She pointed to the sign. "We close at five o'clock."

"It's four fifty-seven," George called out behind me. She held up her wrist, showing the woman her giant watch with multiple dials. "This is a satellite watch. It's accurate to the nanosecond."

Reluctantly the woman opened the door all the way and let us in. "I really must close at five," she said, "but if you girls would like to look around for the next three minutes, you're welcome to."

We walked into the store, which reminded me of the nautical museum, but even more cluttered. Paintings covered the wall from floor to ceiling. There was a corner that was entirely devoted to used books on Nantucket history. A variety of furniture was placed throughout the store, each piece piled high with Nantucket souvenirs—pillows, dishware, pennants—dating back to the 1950s. Behind me Bess coughed, reacting to the dust.

"We're wasting nanoseconds," George whispered.

I realized she was right. We had been standing in the doorway almost dumbstruck, overwhelmed by the vast amount of stuff before us.

"Could you show us where you keep your scrimshaw?" I asked the shopkeeper.

"It's all in that case over there," she said, pointing to a far corner.

We made our way through the store, carefully sticking to the narrow path that had been cleared around the various pieces of furniture.

"This is all just old junk," George said quietly. "Why would anyone buy this stuff?"

"This is not junk," Jenna said tersely. "These are treasures, each with its own story."

George shrugged. Jenna was never going to turn George into a history buff.

We reached the display case with the scrimshaw. It consisted of three shelves, each containing about fifty pieces of ivory. Jenna pulled the museum catalog from her purse and plopped it on top of the counter. She flipped it open to the scrimshaw page. Small photos accompanied descriptions of the pieces in the museum's collection. Someone had drawn red stars next to five of the pieces.

"The ones with the star next to them are the ones that are missing from the museum," she explained.

"That's the one the lady at the museum was wearing," I said, pointing to its picture.

"So we're looking for one of these four?" Bess clarified.

It occurred to me that there were four pieces and

four of us. "Why don't we each look for one piece? That will probably be the fastest way to find them." I could feel the store owner hovering behind us. I knew the minute the clock struck five, she would ask us to leave. The others agreed, and we each picked a carving to look for. Mine featured a design of a seagull soaring over a rough sea.

We all leaned over the case and got to work scanning the scrimshaw for the stolen pieces. We were quiet as we looked. It took a lot of concentration to make sure you saw every piece.

"Found it!" Jenna announced, pointing to a pendant in the back right of the second shelf.

"Can we see that one?" I asked the owner. She sighed but came around and unlocked the case, pulling out the pendant. I checked against the catalog; it was definitely the same artifact.

"Where did you get this?" I asked.

"Someone sold it to us. It's how we acquire everything we sell here," she answered.

"Do you remember who?" I asked hopefully.

"I'm afraid not. This is one of our busiest times of year. People are clearing out their houses as they prepare to close them up for the fall, so we often buy several items a day. It is very hard to keep it all straight."

I bit on my lip, wondering how I could jog her memory. Out of the corner of my eye, I spotted Jenna's museum catalog and got an idea. "You must have some sort of ledger," I said, "where you keep a list of everything you buy and sell."

The woman paused before answering. She knew what I was going to ask next, and she didn't like it. "Yes . . . ," she replied hesitantly.

"Could you please check it for us?" I asked.

"It's late, girls. I really have to go." She sighed, crossing her arms over her chest.

"Please," Jenna begged. "My job depends on it."

The woman looked at Jenna, and I guess she realized just how desperate she was. "Fine," she relented.

"Thank you!" Jenna squealed. The shopkeeper took the pendant and went over to an old computer sitting in the back corner. Jenna, George, Bess, and I waited with baited breath. The big break we were looking for might be coming!

"This piece was brought in by Peter Boyd," the woman finally said.

I couldn't believe it. Beside me George and Bess gasped. I realized I hadn't had a chance to share with any of them what the sisters had told me about Pete's history of publicity stunts. But I was shocked too. I had considered the idea that Pete had temporarily removed the figurehead to sell tickets, but I hadn't thought he might actually be stealing from the museum.

"No," Jenna said firmly. "That can't be right."

"It says so right here," the woman insisted, pointing at her screen.

"There has to be an error," Jenna maintained.

The woman beckoned Jenna over, and we all followed. She held out the pendant. "You see this number in the upper right corner of the price tag?" We nodded. "It corresponds with this number on our spreadsheet. It shows who sold us the item and how much we bought it for. I can also search and see what else the seller brought in." She ran the search. "Peter Boyd brought in five items this summer." She started to describe them, and it quickly became clear that she was describing the five pieces of scrimshaw that were missing from the museum.

Jenna looked as pale as a sheet. Her entire image of Pete had been stripped away.

"I'm sorry, girls," the woman said. "But I have an appointment. I really must close up now."

We shuffled out—except for Bess, who stayed behind to buy an old Nantucket pennant. It was blue felt with a yellow-and-white sailboat painted on it.

"You could have just taken a photo of Jenna's boat," George observed as we stepped outside.

"I think this will look pretty on my wall at home," Bess said. "Besides, I figured we should buy something to thank her for her help."

"I can't believe Pete would steal from the museum," Jenna said.

"I was so certain Kelsey had taken that scrimshaw because she needed the money," Bess added.

"The more I think about it," I said, "the more Pete does make sense as a suspect."

Jenna looked at me sharply. "How so?"

I told them about Pete's lifelong love of publicity stunts. "Also, wouldn't most people in his position insist on calling the police as soon as the figurehead went missing?" I could see the girls thinking about this.

"Maybe he didn't want the police looking into the theft too closely, and he thought Nancy wouldn't be able to figure it out," Bess suggested.

"But if he stole the figurehead to sell it, that's not a publicity stunt," Jenna said. "He loves the museum. It's his whole life."

"But he stole and sold the scrimshaw," I countered, "and the figurehead is worth a lot more."

"I just don't think it's him," Jenna insisted. "Why would he want to hurt the exhibit?"

I sighed. Instead of providing answers, discovering that Pete had stolen the scrimshaw had just raised more questions. Why, for instance, would he want to sabotage Jenna's boat? Maybe the stolen scrimshaw was just a coincidence and had nothing to do with the figurehead. Two independent thefts in one museum over one month seemed unlikely, though. Maybe the threats against Jenna were unrelated to the figurehead? I just couldn't make sense of it!

I was so lost puzzling out the details of the case that it took me a moment to realize that all my friends were staring at me expectantly.

"So, what do we do now, Nancy?" Bess asked.

"I think we have to talk to Pete," I responded. "Tell him we know about the ivory and ask him point-blank about the figurehead."

Jenna sniffled. I looked over and saw that she was no longer fighting her tears. They were streaming down her face. "Excuse me," she said as she rooted around in her purse. "Pete's been my mentor for so long. I just never thought he would be capable of something like this."

I rubbed my hand on Jenna's back to try to comfort her. I couldn't think of anything to say that would make her feel better. It was horrible to find out someone you trust has betrayed you.

"Found a tissue," Jenna said. "Wait a second. This isn't it." She was holding a piece of paper with a note written on it. I watched her read it. Her eyes went wide with fear. "Nancy . . ."

She thrust the piece of paper toward me. I took it from her hand and read:

JENNA, IF YOU DO NOT STOP THIS
EXHIBIT, YOU WILL GET HURT.

CHAPTER TEN

Different Directions

"WHAT DOES IT SAY?" GEORGE DEMANDED. I handed her the note so she could read it for herself. Bess read it over her shoulder.

"If I shut down this exhibit, everything I've worked for is over," Jenna moaned.

"A job isn't worth getting hurt, though," Bess argued.

Jenna sighed. I could tell she didn't necessarily agree with Bess. She had focused on getting this job for so long, it probably did seem more important than her own safety. I thought back to Ned's suggestion that perhaps Jenna had taken the figurehead herself because she couldn't handle the stress of the opening. She did seem to be under a lot of pressure, and I could see wanting to be free of that, but I didn't have enough proof to feel comfortable pursuing that lead over any of the others. If I was wrong and Jenna hadn't done this herself, then I would be leaving her high and dry.

"I know the note is scary, but it's actually a good thing," I said.

"How is it a good thing?" Bess asked.

"It tells us what the culprit wants," I explained.

"Which gives us a motive," George added, catching my drift.

"Right. Up until now we didn't know why the figurehead was stolen," I pointed out. "We didn't know whether it was stolen because someone wanted to humiliate Jenna or perhaps the museum itself, or if it was taken in order to sell it to make money." Bess and Jenna nodded. "Now we know that whoever stole it has something against this particular exhibit," I said.

Bess turned to Jenna. "Who wouldn't want this exhibit to take place?"

"Besides Kelsey," I said. "We still have her on the list, and I know she would benefit from you not getting the job, but we need to broaden our pool of suspects."

Jenna bit her fingernails as she thought. "I can't think of anyone. No one gets hurt by this exhibit. Everyone I feature in it has been dead for at least fifty years."

"Marni told me that some of the people who live here year-round are very protective of the mystery of the *Eleanore Sharpe,* and they wouldn't want you to tell the truth. Is there any islander you can think of who would feel particularly strongly about that?"

Jenna shrugged. "I don't know. I thought all of that was a bit silly, so I didn't pay attention. I'm sorry."

I thought of Marni and how she was related to whaling captains. "What about descendants?" I asked. "Are there any living descendants of the captain who wouldn't want to see his name tarnished?"

Jenna looked at me blankly. "I don't know. My focus is on the past. I never looked into anything like that. It never occurred to me that I might make someone upset. I'm just telling the truth."

I thought Jenna was a little naive to think that simply telling the truth wouldn't upset someone, but now was not the time to argue with her.

I checked my watch. We had just over an hour before the doors opened for the reception and Mr. Whitestone walked through the door to find the figurehead missing. We needed to hurry. The only way forward was to divide and conquer.

"George," I said. "Go to Marni's house and see if you can gather any more information about descendants of the captain or islanders who would be offended by the exhibit."

George nodded. "I'm on it!" she called. Jenna gave her Marni's address, and George headed off, using her phone for directions.

I turned to Bess and Jenna. "We're going back to the museum and talking to Pete."

Jenna sighed. "I really don't think it's Pete. Why would he want the exhibit closed?"

"I don't know, but he knows more than he told us. We can't solve this unless we have all the information," I insisted.

Jenna and Bess agreed, and we headed back to the museum. The sun was setting and it was starting to get dark.

As we approached the museum, we saw a crowd gathered out front, waiting for the doors to open.

"At first I was sad my parents couldn't make it," Jenna said, "but now I'm glad they don't have to see me humiliated in front of all these people."

I felt a stab of guilt. I had promised Jenna I could solve this mystery, and I was letting her down.

"Let's go around back so we don't have to walk through the crowd," Bess suggested.

Jenna and I agreed that this sounded like a good idea. We cut through an alley that led behind the museum. As we rounded the corner, I stopped Bess and Jenna short.

At the end of the alley, a man was sitting in a wheelchair. The captain's hat on his head was a dead giveaway that it was Jeremiah.

"What's he doing here?' Jenna asked.

"He wouldn't want to come to the opening?" I asked.

Jenna shook her head. "You couldn't pay him to come to it. He hates this place. He claims that he breaks out in hives whenever he comes within a block. Says he must be allergic to people who treat history like it's a joke."

"Unless he knows the figurehead won't be here and he wants to see Pete embarrassed," I suggested.

"It looks like he's waiting for someone," Bess said.

"Maybe his partner in crime," I said. "Let's wait here and see who comes out."

We remained hidden around the corner of the alley, only our heads peering around the side. We could quickly jump back if Jeremiah happened to look in our direction. So far he was focused solely on the door to the museum. He tapped his good foot impatiently on the wheelchair's footrest.

"He told us he offered you a job," I said quietly to Jenna.

Jenna nodded. "I thought about taking it," she said.

Bess looked at her, surprised. "Why would you want to work with someone so rude?" she asked.

"He knows more about the history of this island than anyone else. I could have learned a lot from him, but if no one comes to see the exhibits you create, what's the point?"

All of a sudden the door creaked open and a woman walked out carrying a large, heavy bundle.

"That could be the figurehead!" Jenna whispered urgently. "It's about the right size."

The way the light was shining behind them, we could only see the person in silhouette. Besides being female, I couldn't make out any other distinguishing characteristics.

"Who is that?" Bess asked.

"I can't tell," Jenna answered.

"We need to get closer," I said. I led the way, showing Bess and Jenna how to stay close to the wall and walk quickly and quietly without being seen or heard. We took refuge behind a Dumpster halfway down the alley, which gave us a much better view.

"It's Kelsey!" I exclaimed under my breath.

"I knew she was up to no good!" Bess whispered.

"We don't know what is going on," I said. We were still too far away to hear what they were saying, and I wanted to keep an open mind as to what was transpiring between them. One of the worst things a detective can do is jump to conclusions.

Although, I had to admit, it did not look good for Kelsey or Jeremiah.

Jeremiah reached into his pocket, pulled out a wad of cash, and handed it to Kelsey.

"That must be the payment she was talking about at the soda fountain!" Bess whispered.

Kelsey carefully counted the money twice. Finally she nodded, indicating that it was correct. They spoke for a few more seconds, and then Kelsey walked around behind Jeremiah's wheelchair and pushed him down the alley away from us.

"I knew Jeremiah wanted to examine the figurehead himself," Jenna began, "but I didn't think he would stoop to stealing it."

"Maybe he didn't get the idea until Kelsey offered it to him. She would get quick money—which we know she needs—and it would cost Jenna her job," Bess suggested.

It all made sense, but there was something still bugging me. "Why would they tell Jenna to shut down the exhibit?" I asked. "If part of Jeremiah's motive was to embarrass Pete, wouldn't he want the exhibit to open so that everyone knew that Pete lost the figurehead?"

Neither Jenna nor Bess had an answer for that. At the end of the alley, Kelsey and Jeremiah turned right. If we didn't start following them now, we would lose track of them. "You two go after Jeremiah and Kelsey," I said. "Be careful, but find out what they are up to."

"What are you going to do?" Bess asked.

"I'm going to talk to Pete," I said. "There have been so many wrong turns and twists in this case. I want to make sure we cover all our bases."

Jenna and Bess nodded and took off after Jeremiah and Kelsey. I entered the museum through the back door, which had been cleared of visitors and was being prepared for the reception. Tables were set up in the main exhibit hall and covered with white tablecloths. Caterers in white shirts and black vests arranged trays of appetizers. It looked like it would be a really nice event. I just hoped it wouldn't be ruined by this missing figurehead.

I didn't see Pete in the exhibit hall, so I made my way to his office. I was about to knock when I heard voices from inside.

"Won't people notice it's gone?" asked a man's voice I didn't recognize. I leaned in, pushing my ear up against the door as hard as I could. A few of the caterers gave me odd looks. In different circumstances I would try to eavesdrop more discreetly, but right then I didn't have time to worry about appearances.

"Let me worry about that," a voice I instantly recognized as Pete's answered. "It's my museum; I'll take the heat."

"It just seems really risky," the unknown man continued.

"Are you looking at this piece?"

"She's a real beauty," the man conceded, "but I don't know. . . ."

"Do you know what I've risked by arranging this? I could lose my job," Pete said, his voice raised in anger.

"I'm sorry," the other man mumbled. I could barely hear him. "I'll take it. I appreciate everything you've done for me."

Before I knew what was happening, the door flung open and I went flying into Pete's office. I landed sprawled on the floor with a loud *thunk*, right at Pete's feet.

It took a moment for me to get my bearings. My wrists were sore from bracing my fall, but I didn't think I had hurt them badly.

"Nancy!" Pete said angrily. "What were you doing?"

"How much did you hear?" the other man asked. He was tall and broad-shouldered, with deep-set eyes and a pronounced forehead that made him look imposing, especially from my position on the ground. He glared at me furiously, waiting for my answer.

"You took the figurehead," I said to Pete. "And you're selling it to him!" I pointed to the other man.

Before I knew what was happening, the large man stepped over me with one long stride, slamming the door shut. Now I was trapped in Pete's office with two men who clearly didn't want me there. Not only that, but whatever I had walked into seemed sinister.

I stared up at Pete and the other man, waiting for what would happen next.

CHAPTER ELEVEN

A Whale's Tail

TO MY SURPRISE, PETE BURST OUT LAUGHING.
"You think I stole the figurehead?" he asked between
chortles.

"I know you stole the scrimshaw," I said. If anything, Pete laughed even harder. I looked around, per-
plexed. I had no idea what was so funny.

"I didn't steal the scrimshaw, Nancy. It's in my con-
tract that with the permission of the board of trustees,
I can sell museum assets if I think it's necessary."

"Did you get the board's permission?" I asked.

"Of course I did." He reached down to help me

up, but I didn't take his hand right away. I still had questions.

"Then why didn't you tell Kelsey or Jenna?" I asked.

"I don't discuss financial matters with our interns, Nancy," he explained. "I didn't want them to worry. We're getting into our slow season, and I needed some extra money to see us through the winter. I do it every year."

"Shouldn't it have been marked in the catalog, then?" I asked.

"Look at this place," Pete said, sweeping his arm around his cluttered office. "Do you think I'm that organized?"

I had seen how he "organized" his letters, throwing every envelope the museum received into a box. It was easy to believe that he would just forget to update the museum catalog.

Pete offered his hand again, and this time I accepted it. I got to my feet and brushed myself off. "Any more questions?" he asked.

"Yes," I said. "What were you two talking about?" I

indicated the man who had stood silently while I interrogated Pete. "If it wasn't about the figurehead, what was it?"

"I told you it was a bad idea," the other guy said to Pete. "Even this girl could see we were up to no good."

"Allow me to introduce my stepbrother, David," Pete said. David gave a halfhearted wave. "He runs a restoration and authentication business and last year he got in a little trouble," Pete continued. "He sold some items he shouldn't have sold—"

"You sold the illegal whale ivory," I interjected. "It was too new. It had come from whales that were illegally hunted."

David sighed dramatically. "It was one mistake. It was wrong, but I paid my fine, and no one will let me forget it. I haven't been able to get work all summer."

"So," Pete said, "being the good older brother that I am—"

"Stepbrother," David interrupted.

"Being the good older stepbrother I am," Pete conceded, "I'm throwing David some restoration work to help him get back on his feet." He indicated a painting on an easel in the corner. It showed a man standing at the lookout at the top of a ship's mast, pointing to a tiny whale fluke off in the distance as the rest of the crew sprang into motion to go after the whale. One man, who looked strikingly young, stood near the front of the boat looking like he'd been caught off guard, as if he was just realizing what he had gotten himself into. A plaque on the frame read SO IT BEGINS.

Pete and David were right. It was a beautiful painting, but even my untrained eye could see that it needed work to bring it back to its full glory. The colors were faded, and there were cracks in various places.

I looked between them. I didn't really think that Pete still had the figurehead, but I didn't think I was getting the whole story. "If it's so innocent, why were you so concerned that I had heard what you were saying?"

"Okay," Pete said, "it's not completely on the up-and-up. The board is supposed to approve anyone we hire to do restoration."

"With my past, they'll never allow me to do the work," David added.

"But his skills are amazing, and I completely trust him," Pete said. "Once the board sees his work, they will grant approval in the future."

"Please don't say anything, Nancy. I need this," David begged. I didn't know how I felt about what Pete and David were doing, but this was Pete's decision. My focus was on the figurehead—and it was looking less and less likely that Pete had it.

"Aside from Jenna, I have the most riding on this exhibit. I would never do anything to jeopardize it," Pete said. He was right. He didn't have a motive. Once it was clear that he had sold the scrimshaw for the benefit of the museum and not for his own personal gain, I didn't have anything that pointed toward him.

"You're welcome to take a look around my office if you still don't believe me," he offered.

Poking around his office could take hours. "That won't be necessary," I said.

"I'm going to take this painting out the back exit," David said. "Your board is probably waiting to get in." He wrapped up the painting and carried it out.

"Shall we see how the preparations are coming along?" Pete asked me.

"Sure," I said. I couldn't help but feel dispirited. I was fresh out of leads. My phone hadn't rung, so I had no reason to believe that Bess and Jenna had found the figurehead with Jeremiah or that George had gotten any decent information out of Marni.

We walked into the main exhibit hall, which looked amazing. Someone had lined the sperm whale skeleton with Christmas lights, which cast a warm, gentle glow over the entire space.

George, Bess, and Jenna were back, but the looks on their faces confirmed my suspicions that they had gotten nowhere.

"What did Marni say?" I asked George.

"I couldn't find her," George answered. "Her grandfather said she'd already left for dinner before heading over here. I called her a few times, but she didn't answer.

I didn't see her outside, so I guess she's probably still eating."

"What happened with Jeremiah and Kelsey?" I asked Bess and Jenna.

"We lost them," Bess said.

"We got caught behind a wedding party. They took up the whole sidewalk, and we couldn't get around them for two blocks," Jenna explained.

A horn blasted out into the night. "That's the ferry-boat coming in," Jenna said. "The one Mr. Whitestone is on." She looked sad.

"I'm really sorry, Jenna," I apologized. "I thought I could find the figurehead for you."

"It's okay, Nancy," Jenna replied, though she didn't sound like she was okay. She sounded crushed.

"If only I had just a little more time. I know we're close," I said.

"Time is the one thing we don't have," George interjected. "The reception is supposed to start in fifteen minutes."

"There's no way you could show the exhibit

without the figurehead and Nancy could keep working on finding it tomorrow?" Bess asked.

Jenna shook her head. "Without it, all I have is speculation. The figurehead is my proof that the captain deliberately sank the ship. The marks on the figurehead show the angle at which he hit the rocks. Opening the exhibit without the figurehead would be just as bad as not opening it at all."

The four of us sat in silence on a bench in the middle of the room. The sperm whale skeleton hung above us.

I hated to let someone down. It irked me to no end that this thief had outsmarted me. I thought back to the beginning of the case, when I'd been so convinced it would be one of the easier ones I had tackled. If I hadn't been so overconfident, maybe Jenna would have gone to the police and the figurehead would be safely in its display case. I knew it was silly to play the "what-if" game, but I couldn't help it. It felt like this was all my fault.

Pete came over. "Sorry, Jenna. I think I need to

tell everyone that the reception is canceled and start refunding tickets."

Jenna nodded but didn't look up from the floor. I gave Pete an apologetic smile.

Pete headed toward the door. Bess squeezed Jenna's hand.

All of a sudden there was loud *CRACK* above us. Before we could react, the tail of the sperm whale skeleton came crashing down on the floor right in front of us. We all dove for cover, crawling under a nearby table, our hands clasped over our necks to protect our heads. We stayed for a moment, looking at one another, waiting to see if the rest of the skeleton was going to follow the tail to the floor.

After a moment, Pete called, "Come on out. It's safe now." We climbed from under the table and dusted ourselves off.

The tail was scattered across the floor, along with several vertebrae. Looking up, we saw the skeleton still swinging gently. The third cable, the one that had supported the tail, was hanging free.

"You girls okay?" Pete asked. We all nodded. He picked up the tail and inspected it. "It's cracked," he said, "but all things considered, it's in pretty good shape." We picked up the rest of the vertebrae from the floor and handed them to Pete.

I found a piece of the cable lying on the floor and brought it to Pete. "Do you think someone could have cut it?" I asked.

Pete studied it. "It's hard to tell. I'd have to look at it under a microscope."

"Wouldn't you have noticed someone up there with a ladder and a cable cutter?" George asked.

"Most days, yes," Pete replied, "but we had a lot of people in and out today, doing work on various parts of the museum to prep for tonight."

I looked over at Jenna. She was staring at the spot where the tail had landed, her face as white as a sheet.

"That note did say I would be in danger if I didn't cancel the exhibit," Jenna said.

"But you did cancel the exhibit. That's not playing by the rules!" Bess said indignantly.

"The culprit doesn't know that it's canceled," I countered.

All of a sudden, there was another cracking noise, this one much softer than the last. Another vertebra fell from the tail, hitting George right on the top of the head. "Ow! My head!" she cried out.

"George!" Bess exclaimed.

We guided her back to the bench. Pete barked at the caterers to block off the space under the skeleton so no one would stand there.

"How many fingers am I holding up?" Bess asked George, frantically waving three fingers in front of her face.

"I don't have a concussion, Bess. This was barely a knock. It just surprised me."

"Answer the question," Bess insisted.

"Three!" George answered. "Satisfied?"

"Not really," Bess said. "I think we should take you to the hospital. Two knocks to the head in one day can't be good."

George brushed off Bess's concerns. "It barely even

hurts. I haven't felt dizzy or sick to my stomach or anything the nurse said to look out for." She turned to Jenna. "But I am going to demand more of those doughnuts as payment. Twice now I've taken knocks to the head that were meant for you."

Jenna looked at George, confused. "When was the first time?" she asked. I realized that amid the busyness of the afternoon we had never told Jenna about the incident on the boat. We gave her a quick rundown.

Jenna still looked confused when we finished explaining what had happened. "But why do you think I was the target of the sabotage, not Marni?" she asked.

"Because no one knew that you had lent Marni your boat," I said.

"Everyone knew that," Jenna said.

"What do you mean?" I asked.

"There was an article about our so-called 'unusual' friendship in the newspaper just last week, because I'm a summer person and Marni is a full-time islander. One of the examples they used was how my family had lent Marni our boat for the fall regatta," she said.

"I can't believe I didn't double-check what she said online," George admonished herself. "Maybe I do have a concussion. I'm slipping."

Suddenly it all started to click like fireworks going off in my mind as the pieces finally started snapping into place.

I turned to Pete. "Can you get this all cleaned up and the skeleton stabilized in the next twenty minutes?" I asked.

Pete nodded. "If Jenna helps me."

"Great," I said. "Tell everyone you're running a little late, but the exhibit will be open in half an hour."

"Nancy," Jenna said. "What are you doing?"

"Come on," I told Bess and George. "I know where the figurehead is!"

CHAPTER TWELVE

⌒

A Race
Against Time

I RACED OUT THE BACK OF THE MUSEUM, Bess and George right on my heels. The three of us sprinted down the alley toward Broad Street.

"Nancy, where are we going?" George panted behind me.

I didn't have the breath to answer, so I just kept running. They'd see soon enough.

We hit Broad Street and turned onto Beach Street. The seven p.m. ferry that had just arrived had filled the sidewalks with people wheeling suitcases. Taxicabs clogged the street, slowing our progress, but I would not be deterred.

"Excuse me, coming through. Pardon me," I announced as I weaved between families and zigzagged around groups of friends congesting the narrow path. I heard my friends echoing the same words behind me.

Finally we made it to the Sailing Club. I barged through the doors, Bess and George following me. Fred was still sitting behind the counter.

"Good evening, Fred," I said authoritatively as we marched past him.

"Wait," he shouted after us. "You can't come in here!" But we didn't slow down. I didn't have time to haggle about permission to enter. Maybe tomorrow when this was over we could stop by with a box of doughnuts to make it up to him. But right now we were on a mission.

As I pushed open the door from the main room to the outside patio, I ran smack into Connor.

"Nancy!" he exclaimed.

"Hi, Connor," I said as I tried to get past him, but every direction I stepped, he stepped too, blocking me from getting around him. We carried on like this for a few seconds, as if we were performing an awkward dance.

"Connor, I'm in a hurry," I said, exasperated, but Connor refused to let me go by.

"I just got a text from Kelsey," he mentioned. "She said that the skeleton fell at the museum. Is Jenna okay?"

"She's fine," I replied, trying once again to get around him, but Connor was quicker than I was. He put his hands on my shoulders, forcing me to pay attention to him.

"If I had known Jenna was in actual danger, I never would have vandalized the sign. You know that, right? It was just a stupid prank," he insisted.

I took a deep breath and looked him right in the eyes. "I know that," I said. "Right now, I have to go so I can save her exhibit . . . and her career."

"I want to help," he said.

"Fine," I said. At this point, it was easier to let him tag along than waste any more time arguing.

"Great!" he shouted, letting go of my shoulders and allowing me to pass.

I picked up my pace and led everyone to the docks and down to the last slip, where Jenna's boat had been earlier in the day. But it was gone.

"Where is it?" I blurted out.

"Is that it?" George asked, pointing into the distance. I followed her finger and spotted a boat bobbing right where the calm water of the harbor transitioned into open ocean.

"It's too far," I said. "I can't tell."

"That's Jenna's boat," Connor said next to me.

"How can you tell?" Bess asked.

"I recognize the silhouette," he said. "Just trust me, I'm really good at boats, and that is Jenna's."

"Do you really want to help Jenna?" I asked Connor. "Do you want to do something that will make it up to her for destroying her sign?"

"Anything," Connor said. Jenna's boat was going

farther and farther out to sea. We needed to move quickly.

"Take us out to that boat. Now."

Connor nodded. "Follow me," he said. "We have to move fast." He led us down to the opposite end of the dock to a boat named *Stingray*. It was smaller than Jenna's. I hoped Connor was a good enough sailor to make up the distance.

"This is it," Connor said. We all quickly put on life jackets and climbed into the boat, which started to tilt precariously. "Nancy, Bess, get on the other side," Connor ordered. Bess and I slid to the opposite side, and the boat righted itself. "We have to keep the boat balanced," he said sternly.

I looked out to see Jenna's boat drifting farther away. "We need to hurry!" I exclaimed.

Connor pulled the cover over the sail and started hoisting it up the mast. He moved quickly and efficiently. "Hold this," he told me as he handed me the till. He climbed over Bess and George back onto the dock and pushed us off, jumping back into the boat at the last minute. He took the till back from me.

"Pay attention and do as I say," Connor directed. He worked us through the harbor. The area was secluded, and there was barely even a breeze. Connor jumped from side to side, controlling the boom and the till, maneuvering us around the boats and out into the open ocean.

It was slow going, but finally we made our way to the edge of the harbor and caught the wind. Suddenly we were cutting through the water. "Woo-hoo!" Connor yelled. "I love this moment!"

It was definitely an adrenaline rush to feel the wind blowing the boat, pushing it over the waves. It rocked back and forth and dipped up and down as we sped over the water. This was definitely more exciting than the sailing I had done on the lake at camp.

Bess, on the other hand, looked a little green. "Just watch the horizon," I told her. I had learned at summer camp that keeping your eyes focused on the evenness of the horizon could help if you were feeling seasick. Bess nodded.

"It looks like Jenna's boat stopped moving," George observed.

Jenna's boat did look anchored. It was bobbing in the ocean, but not actually moving forward. Someone stood at the bow.

"Connor, can you cut around in front of it?" I asked.

"Sure thing," Connor agreed. He brought us around front, and we had a clear view of Marni teetering on the edge of the boat, holding the figurehead. All she had to do was let go and it would sink into the sea.

"Go away, Nancy," Marni called out tearfully. "You can't stop me."

"I know why you did it," I said. "I understand, but this isn't the right way."

"How can you know?" she asked.

"Your grandfather's grandfather was the captain who sank the *Eleanore Sharpe*," I said.

Bess and George gasped. Marni looked at me, almost relieved that someone understood.

"Jenna set up this sneak peek tour of the exhibit

for me and my grandfather on Friday afternoon, just before you guys got here. She had to leave to meet you at the ferry, and then Grandpa started to get so upset. He's supposed to be careful, but he wouldn't calm down. I was so scared that he would give himself a heart attack. He just kept yelling that this was a disgrace and we had to stop it. I didn't know what to do. I'd never seen him like that before. I saw Kelsey's purse with her keys and I decided the easiest thing would be to stop the exhibit. I stole the figurehead, wrapped it in an old blanket, and hid it in his wheelchair."

"Why didn't you just talk to Jenna?" I asked.

"She wouldn't have understood. She would have said she was just telling the truth."

That seemed a little unfair to Jenna, but I could see why Marni would think that. Tears were streaming down her cheeks.

"You didn't have to clock me on the head," George said angrily.

"I know," Marni wailed. "Everything just got out of

control. I didn't want my grandfather to get in trouble. He's so fragile." She turned to George, who was still watching her with her arms crossed over her chest, unmoved by Marni's explanation. "I'm sorry I hit you with the boom, George. I didn't mean to. You were just so close to the figurehead, I got flustered and the rope slipped." Marni let out a loud sob that carried in the wind, becoming a sad, haunting sound.

"I don't know what to do. I don't want to hurt Jenna. She's my friend, but I can't let her hurt my grandfather," Marni wept.

"If you didn't want to hurt Jenna, why'd you cut the cable to the whale skeleton?" Bess asked, still angry. "You could have killed someone!"

Marni stopped crying for a second and looked up, confused. "What are you talking about? I didn't touch the skeleton."

"You left a note in her purse, saying she'd be hurt if she didn't stop the exhibit, and thirty minutes later the skeleton fell," George said.

"I left that note, but I was just trying to scare her.

I didn't know what else to do! I would never actually hurt Jenna!" Marni wailed.

I didn't know what to believe, but we could sort that out later. Right now I needed to get the figurehead back.

"Can you get us alongside her boat?" I asked Connor.

"I can try," he said. Slowly he maneuvered our boat so that it was parallel to Marni's.

"A little closer?" I asked Connor. Marni was still bawling. I was worried that she was so swept up in her emotions that she would let go of the figurehead and it would tumble into the ocean, sinking to the bottom.

"That's as close as I can get," Connor said. We were about a foot away from Marni's boat.

I stood up and checked my life jacket, which fit snugly against my chest. "Switch sides with me," I said to George. We changed spots, so now I was right next to Marni's boat.

"What are you doing, Nancy?" Bess asked with a nervous tone in her voice. I knew she'd try to talk me out of what I was about to do if I explained it to her, but I didn't see any other options.

"Getting back the figurehead," I told her. I stood up on the edge of the boat, working hard to keep my balance. Marni's boat was about a foot taller than Connor's.

"I don't think I like this," George said, but I was determined.

"Hold it steady," I told Connor.

"I'll do my best," he answered.

I took a deep breath and leaped. With the sway of the boat, I wasn't able to push off as strongly as I needed. My right foot hooked on the edge of Marni's boat, and I landed on her deck with a *thunk*. I cringed, expecting to hear a splash as the figurehead hit the water, but it never came.

"Nancy! Are you okay?" Bess called from the other boat.

"I'm fine," I answered. I brushed myself off and made my way to the bow of the boat, where Marni was still sobbing. I had a feeling that, left on her own, she would be crying for a long time.

"Marni," I said gently. "Hand me the figurehead."

"I can't," she said through tears.

"There's nothing you've done that can't be fixed. George is fine. Jenna is fine. If you give me the figurehead right now, we can get it back before they open the doors to the reception. No one will ever know it was gone."

Marni looked up. She stopped crying for a moment and I could see a look of hope in her eyes, but then her face crumpled and she let out another wail. "But my grandfather . . . ," she said.

"Your grandfather's a tough man. No one makes it to a hundred and four without being strong. He can take this." Marni didn't look convinced. "Besides," I continued, "I bet he would rather see this exhibit go up than see you get in trouble." I could see in her eyes that I had gotten through. I extended my arms again. "Just give me the figurehead and this can all be over."

Slowly Marni handed me the figurehead. I breathed a huge sigh of relief and held it tight. Carefully I carried it belowdecks. I didn't want there to be any possibility of something happening to it now.

When I got back up, Marni was curled into a ball, crying. Just by looking at her, I knew that she was not going to be able to sail the boat back to harbor. Before I could contemplate what to do next, I heard the sound of motors. Bright lights were suddenly shining on us. We were surrounded by boats marked UNITED STATES COAST GUARD.

"We received a distress call," a voiced boomed over a loudspeaker.

"That was me," I heard George yell from Connor's boat. "I called you!"

"My friend is in no condition to sail us back," I shouted.

"Coming aboard," the voice echoed through the speaker, and a young, handsome coast guard member boarded our boat.

"I'm Seaman Scott," he introduced himself. "Does she need medical attention?" he asked, indicating Marni.

"No," I said. "Just some rest. She's had a really rough day." He seemed to accept that and quickly took the helm, navigating us back to the Sailing Club docks. Connor followed us back.

I realized how exhausted I was from the whole ordeal. I sat down next to Marni and enjoyed feeling the wind in my hair as we made our way back to land.

Just as we pulled into the harbor, Marni squeezed my hand. "Thanks, Nancy." I squeezed her hand back.

Pete and Jenna met us at the Sailing Club. Apparently, George had called them too. I handed the figurehead back to Jenna, who cradled it like a baby. She looked at me, her eyes glistening with tears of joy. "Nancy, I can't thank you enough," she said.

"No problem," I said. "I'm glad I could help."

Pete clapped me on the shoulder. "Very impressive, Nancy. I can see why you have the reputation you do back home."

I blushed. Compliments make me uncomfortable. All of a sudden, I thought of something. "Pete, Marni told me that she didn't touch the skeleton. Could that be true?"

Pete and Jenna exchanged a look. "Actually, as

we were cleaning up, I looked at the cable under the microscope. I didn't see any evidence that anyone had tampered with it. I think it was an accident. We are very lucky that no one was hurt."

I breathed a sigh of relief, glad that Marni hadn't put anyone in danger.

"Shouldn't you get that back to the museum?" I asked Pete and Jenna, indicating the figurehead.

"We certainly should!" Pete said.

The two of them took off, and Bess, George, and I stayed behind. Bess found the nurse, who agreed to let Marni lie down for a while before she went home. We watched as the nurse escorted Marni to her office.

"She made some really bad decisions over the past thirty-six hours," I said, "but in her own way she was trying to do what she thought was right."

George and Bess nodded. "It's hard to be mad at her," Bess said. "She wanted to protect her family."

"You weren't the one who got hit on the head," George protested. After a beat, she continued. "I'm kidding. I'm not really mad at her. Being caught between your friends and your family is never easy."

We stood quietly for a moment. "Should we head to this reception?" I asked. George and Bess heartily agreed.

By the time we arrived at the museum, the opening was in full swing. The place was filled to capacity. People were hovering in groups, sipping champagne, eating hors d'oeuvres, and happily chatting with one another. I overheard more than one person say that they had been blown away by the exhibit. You'd never guess that less than an hour ago the whole event had been in jeopardy.

"Let's find Jenna and congratulate her," Bess said shouted over all the talking.

George and I nodded. It was hard to spot anyone in the packed room.

"When artists have an opening, they usually stand next to their work," I said. "I wonder if it's the same for curators."

"Should we try the exhibit room first, then?" George asked.

Bess and I agreed. We fought our way to the exhibit room, squeezing past the other guests, murmuring, "Excuse me" over and over again as we made our way through.

When we arrived at the exhibit room, I spied Jenna talking to an older gentleman in a tuxedo in front of the display case that housed the figurehead. I realized that even though I had held the figurehead in my hands, I hadn't really looked at it. I had been too focused on making sure it was returned safely to take the time to carefully examine it. In the display, under the shining lights, it was truly beautiful.

We hurried to greet Jenna, but at the last moment I noticed that the man she was chatting with was wearing a pin on the lapel of his jacket with the initials R.W.

"Wait," I hissed, stopping George and Bess in their tracks. "What's Mr. Whitestone's first name?"

"Roger," George quickly answered. "I saw his bio on the museum's website."

I pointed to his pin. "I think that's him," I whispered. "Let's not go over until they've finished talking."

We hung back and watched. It was too loud to hear

what they were saying, but after a moment they shook hands, and Jenna's face erupted into a huge smile. As soon as Mr. Whitestone walked away, we rushed over to Jenna.

"What did he say?" Bess asked.

"Did you get the job?" George piped up before Jenna even had a chance to answer the first question.

"I did!" Jenna gushed. "I got the job!" We embraced her in a giant group hug. "Mr. Whitestone said this was one of the best exhibits he has seen curated by someone of any age, and he would be thrilled if I worked here full-time."

"That's so great!" I said.

"You deserve it," added Bess.

"Thank you," Jenna said. "But I couldn't have done it without all your help."

"It was my pleasure," I said.

"Ooh, mini quiches!" George squealed, eyeing a waiter walking by with a tray. We all laughed at how completely she had broken the sentimental mood.

"I'm still feeling a little queasy from the boat ride," Bess said.

"Well, I'm starving!" George said, trailing after the waiter.

"Oh, there's Kelsey," Jenna said, pointing where Kelsey was standing across the room. "Let's go congratulate her."

Bess and I looked at each other, confused. "Congratulate her for what?" I asked.

"She's starting her own business," Jenna explained as we crossed to Kelsey. "She told Pete right before he opened the doors for the reception."

She embraced Kelsey in a hug. "Congratulations!" Jenna said. "I know we had our differences this summer, but I hope we can put them behind us."

Kelsey nodded. "I'm sorry I was such a jerk. I was under a lot of stress and I took it out on you, which wasn't fair. Besides, I couldn't help overhearing your conversation with Mr. Whitestone. You're officially going to be a full-time islander!" Jenna nodded gratefully.

"What is your new business, if I may ask?" I asked.

"I'm dealing antiques!" Kelsey said excitedly. "I've

been saving my money for the past year, and I just signed a lease for a space this week. In fact, today I finalized my first sale to Jeremiah Butler at the historical society."

"That's what you were doing in the alley!" I blurted out. "Completing the sale."

"Yeah . . . ," Kelsey said, obviously surprised that I had seen that exchange.

"That's great!" Bess said. "That seems like a perfect fit for you."

Just then I let out a huge yawn. "I'm so sorry!" I said, embarrassed.

"I'm tired too," Bess said. "Perhaps we should think about going home and going to bed early. I have a big day planned for us tomorrow."

"You do?" I asked.

"It's our last full day on the island," Bess said, "and I plan on beaching, hiking, and shopping! A full vacation in a day," she said with a laugh.

"Yeah, I'm definitely going to need a good night's sleep," I said.

We said our good-byes, pried George away from the appetizers, and made our way back to Jenna's house.

Two days later we were headed back to River Heights. Jenna waited with us at the ferry terminal. It was early in the morning, and there was a bite in the air. It officially felt like fall.

"I talked to Marni," Jenna said. "She's going to work at the museum for free to make up for what she did."

"That sounds fair," I said.

"She's also going to add a section to my exhibit about everything her great-great-grandfather did for the island."

"That is very generous of you," Bess said.

"In this weird way, I'm grateful to her," Jenna said.

"Why?" George asked incredulously.

"I think it was good for someone to teach me that the past isn't just the past. It affects the present. I don't know if I would have learned that without her, and I think it will make me a better curator . . . and person."

George nodded. I wasn't sure if she completely agreed with Jenna's assessment, but she seemed to respect it.

"Now boarding, ferry to Hyannis!" a voice boomed over a loudspeaker.

"That's us!" George said.

We hugged Jenna one last time and made our way up the gangplank to the ferry, waving good-bye as we walked.

A few minutes after we had shoved off, we noticed all the other passengers gathering on the left side of the boat.

"What's going on?' Bess wondered aloud.

"We're getting ready to throw our pennies," a woman carrying a toddler answered, overhearing Bess's question.

"What do you mean?" I asked.

"As we pass by the lighthouse, we each throw a penny and make a wish," she explained.

As we joined the other passengers on deck, I rummaged through my purse for three pennies. I found them just in time, handing one each to George and Bess as we glided by the lighthouse.

I took a deep breath and threw my penny. I knew exactly what my wish was without even having to think about it.

"What did you guys wish for?" George asked.

"We can't tell you that!" Bess said.

"Yeah," I said. "Then it will never come true."

George sulked, but after a moment she perked up. "Is that a whale!?" she shouted. I followed where she was looking, just in time to see a whale in the distance breach and land back in the water with a splash.

I smiled. My wish had come true.

Dear Diary,

SO MAYBE IT WASN'T THE VACATION I imagined, but I do love a good mystery, and this was definitely one of those! In a way, I feel like I know Nantucket better after finding the figurehead than if I had just done the usual tourist activities. I never would have known about the tension between people who visit for the summer and those who live there year-round, for instance. Who knew such a small island could be so complicated?

It's sad that Marni didn't try to talk to Jenna about the exhibit, but she was scared for her grandfather and she panicked. I think Jenna is right, though. What she learned will make her a better museum curator in the future. It's important to remember that the past doesn't just stay in the past; it also affects the present.

"*Keeper of the Lost Cities* is a little bit *Alice's Adventures in Wonderland*, a little bit *Lord of the Rings*, and a little bit *Harry Potter*. And it's all fun!"

—MICHAEL BUCKLEY,
New York Times bestselling author of the Sisters Grimm and NERDS series

"A delightful and dangerous adventure with complex characters and relationships you'll root for to the end of time."

—LISA McMANN,
New York Times bestselling author of *The Unwanteds*, on *Keeper of the Lost Cities*

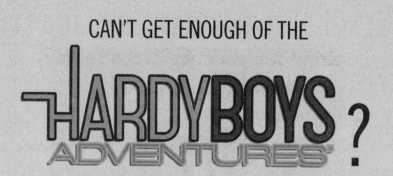

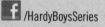